Black River

Louise Walsh

First published in 2016

ISBN: 978-1-84527-590-7

Published with the financial support
of the Welsh Books Council

Cover image: Sarah Richards

Published by Gwasg Carreg Gwalch,
12 Iard yr Orsaf, Llanrwst, Dyffryn Conwy, Cymru LL26 0EH.
tel: 01492 642031
fax: 01492 642502
email: books@carreg-gwalch.com
website: www.carreg-gwalch.com

For Lily, Tommy, Bebel and Jorge

and

for my dear friend Martin Shipton,
for his endless encouragement and support:

'*Ah! Puisque je retrouve un ami si fidèle,*
Ma fortune va prendre une face nouvelle!'

Jean Racine

Chapter 1

"Another tip slide?" Harry said. "Bloody NCB. Every year. Tip slide in '63, then the piece I wrote in '64. You'd have thought they'd have done something about it after last year. Do you remember? Just about every drain in Aberfan was choked with tip slurry."

"Sounds serious this time."

"Could be."

"You'd better get going."

Harry pulled on his coat and stared at Huw on the newsdesk. Huw's primary job was assigning stories, but he spent a good deal of time mediating whenever one of the editors kicked off. Harry read a determination in his colleague's deliberate perusal of newspapers not to hold him up in conversation.

"All anyone does in this country is write letters for the NCB to ignore," Harry said as he made his exit.

In the short walk along Aberfan Road after arriving at the village, Harry found himself tramping through the streams of dirty water flowing down the street and disoriented by thick fog. People were looming up on all sides and disappearing again. Goosebumps broke out across his shoulders and forearms. Unpredictable noises and disconnected, disconcerting sounds gave him a cold sense of fear and dizziness. There was a potent smell of wet mud in the air, but it was different from the smell of a garden after rain. It was the kind of smell that came from building sites and foundations: old underground water and newly oxygenated clay.

He couldn't make up his mind whether the fog was getting thicker. The scream of a claxon made him start. The world and

Harry were swallowed again, but as the fog lifted in places, the emerging scene stopped him short. Hundreds of men were scrabbling and clawing at a hill of greyish black sludge. It was beyond anything he had imagined, unnatural and inexplicable. Harry rejected the phrase 'tip slide'. What had happened deserved another name, something uglier. He shivered and continued to stare at the countless people combing through the sludge with their hands or whatever tools they could find. The horror of it washed over him.

"It's on the school," said an old woman, emerging from the mist. "They're looking for children."

The woman was caught up in a passing group of rescuers and vanished before Harry had a chance to find out if she was all right. He grabbed a policeman who was hurrying past and asked what he could do to help.

"Stay out of the way, please. We've got too many. Even the Territorial Army are held back."

The last of the fog gave way to rain. Harry watched as a young man, desperate to help, attempted to relieve an elderly rescuer of his shovel. The older man's grip proved no tighter than the little claws of a bird on a washing line. All Harry wanted was to help find a child. What he didn't want to do was start interviewing these people.

After an hour or two of observing, he noticed a different kind of person turning up. Wet spectators watched silently and pressed against the digging volunteers in growing numbers. He turned away, disgusted by such savage curiosity and the callousness of those who saw their chance to be part of history.

Harry let his eyes travel the length of Moy Road. He frowned and turned his head to the left a fraction as though listening intently, but he was actually straining to see. There were a number of journalists arriving – outsiders. With them marched photographers loaded down with hard camera bags and multiple cameras on shoulder straps. Immediately, the reporters got to work, stopping those watching and pulling out notebooks. Their pens followed, each clicked on with businesslike tap against the pages.

One journalist in particular caught Harry's eye. He was a deal younger than himself, and his caramel leather coat stood out against the sludge in the same way gorse blossom blazes even brighter before a stormy sky. More than that, he had the manner of a celebrity, introducing himself and shaking hands with the villagers. He appeared to be doling out condolences, trying to measure who was worth talking to by their response. The locals appeared, from where Harry was standing, to blink and stare, possibly wondering whether this man was someone famous. Harry didn't recognise him but he recognised the type. It took him right back to Fleet Street. This reporter, he decided as he tracked him from a distance, was the epitome of everything he hated about London journalism. Although he realised that he wasn't acting rationally among the chaos and devastation, he couldn't bring himself to stop following.

Having little to do other than dwell on the trauma of the situation and join in the cheering when a child was recovered and blankets called for, Harry continued to observe the endless line of journalists pouring in, overflowing from the Mackintosh Hotel and crowding the pubs.

"What did he want?" Harry said to a girl who'd been approached by the Fleet Street journalist.

"He asked me if I knew anyone involved."

"And what did you say?"

"I don't know anyone. I'm from Aberdare. I wanted to see if I could help. Terrible though, isn't it?"

Harry patted her shoulder and frowned as the caramel coat was lost for a few minutes, but he trusted that the journalist hadn't changed course. The rescuers had made some progress clearing the slip in one area. The result was a vast ledge on which the journalist and a photographer eventually appeared, calling down to the rescuers below for information.

Things seemed eerily noiseless to Harry as he reflected on

the scale of the scene. The only sounds to punctuate the silence were those of mass manual labour: digging, coughs, puffing and the odd shout. He cursed the blackish-grey slurry and he considered, momentarily, turning back. He could see from the curve of the area where he was heading how precarious it was – a composite of coal silt and the mud, grass, roots, stones and rubble which it had dragged with it. The vertical edge was incised with the cut lines of spades and gouges where stones had come away with the digging. Harry heaved his feet from the sucking, solidifying mess and tried with great difficulty to stay upright as people clambered past. Anxiety grew in him that he was potentially walking over bodies without knowing it.

The photographer's flash popped what seemed like every three seconds. Harry had the feeling of being in a village destroyed by a violent storm. He could see that the policeman pitching in at the front of the digging – tall and young – was too exhausted to shout at the photographer to stop.

"Can we get down there?" the leather-coated journalist said to the officer, folding his arms as he considered it.

The young policeman didn't answer. He appeared to have found another child – two together, possibly. Aware of the journalist and photographer above him, the policeman ushered his colleagues into a huddle and whispered for them to send the message back for blankets. As Harry neared the edge, he saw the officer sink to sit on his heels as though resting. Harry felt a surge of sympathy for him. He was too young to be dealing with this. The boy reminded Harry of soldiers who had lied about their age, desperate for adventure, only to get blown to bits in some ditch in France.

"We're coming down," the Fleet Street journalist said, looking for a route and interrupting the policeman's contemplation.

"No. You stay there. You'll move the slip!"

"Try that way," the journalist said, nudging his photographer.

"Why don't you try it?" the photographer said, fishing in his pockets.

It was just as the photographer finished cleaning his lens with a rag that Harry caught up with him and the journalist. Harry snatched at a caramel leather sleeve to steady himself and get the journalist's attention.

"Let people do their job," he said, panting.

"Let me do mine. Who the hell are you, anyway?"

As the journalist in the leather coat shrugged Harry's hand away and the policeman seized hold of a blanket, the ledge gave way. The black sludge collapsed over the policeman and the child or children. With it poured greyish water which dislodged further slurry. Harry, the journalist, the photographer and four bystanders fell and lay prostrate, blinking and mud-splattered but largely unhurt, though Harry quickly became aware of pain in his ankle and knee. The guilty group helped each other to their feet and gazed in horror at what had happened. The photographer fussed over his camera as rescuers swore and cleared the muck from the policeman.

"Sorry about that, mate," the journalist said to the filthy, breathless policeman.

"It'll take us about half an hour now," the policeman said, trying to straighten his helmet. "Half an hour to get it all clear and get back to them. You idiots!"

"You said them? There's more than one?"

"Fuck off," the policeman said.

Harry, watching the exchange, wondered whether he had hampered the recovery. To compensate somehow he started trying to clear the slurry with his hands. The desperation was apparent in his frenzied scrabbling at the mud. It was useless. He needed a shovel and looked around for anything that would assist him.

"It was his fault," the Fleet Street journalist said, pointing at Harry. "If he hadn't arrived and started pulling at me..."

The policeman realised that Harry was trying to dig for the

children and threw him off, probably thinking he was doing it to get a picture. Harry fell back in the mud, defeated and humiliated.

"You're like vultures, the lot of you!"

The photographer squeezed back into the pressing crowds, protecting his camera, and the Fleet Street journalist quickly followed. Harry also stepped back and disappeared into the recovery, reddened with cold and the sting of the policeman's damning judgement.

Chapter 2

Harry limped after the flash coat. The Welsh journalist's eyes were bright with anger and his cheeks still burning.

"I'm complaining to the Press Council," he shouted.

The Fleet Street journalist ignored him. Harry winced as he stumbled and pain shot through his knee. The younger journalist continued his retreat without turning around, but then he abruptly changed his mind. He stopped and faced Harry.

"For goodness' sake! A complaint about what? You almost killed the lot of us."

"You what?"

"It's less a press problem and more a 'somebody needs to lose some weight' problem."

The pause was long enough to allow Harry to get a little closer through the crowds and point back in the direction he had come. He ignored the personal comment.

"You were harassing the policeman. Those rescuers. It was you—"

"If you'd left us alone, I would have got the story and my associate John would have got his picture."

Harry threw up his hands in despair, too revolted to say anything.

"Look, don't let's get on like this. We're on the same side, after all. The name's Paul Falstone."

Falstone extended a mud-smeared hand. Harry's fists were pressed to his thighs in an effort to stop them shaking. He longed to sit down with a cup of tea or something stronger.

"I don't care what your name is."

"What paper are you with?"

"I work for the *South Wales Echo* and I would never—"

"Regional papers? You want to work in Fleet Street, mate. Maybe they allow you to hang back in Wales. If I didn't know better, I'd say you were trying to poach my story."

"I was trying to stop you harassing the bereaved."

"Did anyone complain other than you? It's chaos."

Harry looked about him. Light was fading on a warzone. Fine drizzle was again turning to heavy rain. There were countless people working or watching. JCBs battled to divert the slurry still flowing from the mountain. A woman bumped past him with a handkerchief pressed tightly to her mouth, crying silently.

"Look, Taffy," the reporter said, spotting the woman with the handkerchief, "why don't we team up? I was speaking to one of the mothers earlier. She might have opened up if I'd been a bit more Welshy." Falstone, who had adopted an annoying singsong Welsh tone merely in the hope of relieving the tension, finished the sentence by nodding towards the woman who had just walked past, as though they might pounce on her together. "What do you say, mate?"

Harry stared at him, his hands still clenched.

"Fine," Falstone said, seeing he was getting nowhere. A moment later, the journalist was gone.

Harry's legs felt weak, as though he hadn't eaten for days. Exhaustion hung off him like a weighted vest, gripping him under the arms and around his shoulders. He realised he was dangerously close to the deadline for the first edition of that day's *Echo*. He spoke briefly to a senior officer from the fire service who gave him enough factual material to phone something across. After waiting impatiently for a phone line at the Mackintosh Hotel, he promised the copytaker he would have a lot more in an hour or two.

"I don't know how they'll get over it," Harry said, once the main body of the story had been taken. "The cheering when they pull a child out alive is like a Welsh rugby win. Chokes you up. The child's innocent acceptance: worried about their felt-

14

tip pens, what their mum will say about their new shoes being ruined. Time's ticking. The mountain's threatening to slip again. We'll never be the same after this."

Following the call, he used the hotel toilets to splash some water on his face. He leaned on the sink and stared at his dripping reflection. Blinking back at him was a pallid and deeply unhappy old man. He gave a sigh of despair and dried himself before returning to the devastation. He couldn't help wondering where the journalists had been before all of this.

Hours later, human chains of men, some wobbling with fatigue, were passing troughs of slurry on corrugated iron forward down the lines. Standing ponds of water from the two burst water mains had made the spill even more difficult to navigate. Harry rubbed his knee; it was stiffening up. He came across a driverless bulldozer, half buried. There were rumours that the tip was still moving. He didn't expect the queue to identify the deceased at Bethania Chapel would have gone down by much.

The amount of reporters and photographers seemed to have multiplied. They were all interviewing people or creeping and hopping over the spill. Something was going on to Harry's left, too far away for him to get to quickly. Blocking his view was a score of photographers, no doubt taking pictures of a rescue or bereaved parent.

In the back of Harry's mind he felt the pressure of knowing that George, his rival on the *Echo*'s sister paper, the *Western Mail*, with its later deadline, was still around conducting interview after interview. He knew from his earlier call that the names of victims being added to the blackboard in the office was growing and he had yet to contribute anything.

Harry wondered where his *Echo* and *Western Mail* colleagues were situated in the melee, but he knew that the flares and flashes of light from the press cameras were mainly from Fleet Street. How he wished that they could be kept out. They bullied the bereaved and dragged their stories out of them. He alternated between wanting to be invisible to the villagers and wanting to dwarf Fleet Street competition. He mused on the idea of Welsh journalists for Wales. Unable to satisfactorily articulate his thoughts, he found a more secure purchase on the spill and turned his attention to the question he had been hearing all day. Where was God? If there was one, what the hell did God have against children? His next realisation was that he was going to miss his latest deadline. There was no way that he could get to a phone in time to catch the next edition.

He was going to be in serious trouble.

Chapter 3

As the day wore on and the scale of the Aberfan disaster sank in, Harry wrestled with the fact that he had committed a cardinal sin in journalism. He had missed the late afternoon deadline for phoning copy across. The only excuse he would be able to give his editor was that all the phone lines had been tied up with the rescue services. It was hardly going to appease Evan, but the situation wasn't completely irreversible. If Harry stayed overnight, working on a number of stories, he could maintain that while the phone lines had been jammed, he had all the copy the *Echo* could want for its Saturday edition.

Where would he start? Harry felt defeated, but an idea occurred to him. He didn't necessarily have to doorstop the bereaved. Comments from the hundreds of rescuers would be just as valuable. Many of the miners had worked an entire shift underground before they turned their picks and shovels to the rescue. After receiving respite from the immediate horror, perhaps they would willingly share their experiences.

From Harry's initial discussion with the senior fire officer, he knew that there were four main rest and food centres: the Miner's Welfare Hall, the Aberfan Cinema, the Welsh Baptist Church and Smyrna Chapel. He decided on the cinema simply because, when he had passed the worn billboard outside it earlier in the day, there had been advertisements for the *Western Mail* and *Echo* under the latest film posters: a good omen.

By the time he headed in the direction of the cinema, it was early evening. He had missed his deadline and time was racing by in large chunks. What had he been doing? His teeth were chattering. He clamped them together and shivered as, around him, emergency lighting was strung up on poles. When he cut through the crowds towards the rest centre, the arc lights blurred into kaleidoscopic stars rotating like wheels in the mist and rain.

Outside the cinema, a group of rescuers were smoking and talking while a Civil Defence lady attacked the foyer and pavement with a mop and bucket that stank of disinfectant. The carpet inside was soiled with muddy footprints. Shovels and spades leaned against one wall. Harry passed two women heading out into the twilight. They were carrying cinema trays piled high with milk cartons, chocolate and packets of cigarettes – bananas slung over their shoulders. From a room to the left, he could hear utensils banging and the sound of women talking.

A sign on one of the double doors to the cinema itself read, 'Quiet Please. Men Sleeping'. Harry pushed through. The lights were low to enable the volunteers to rest for a few hours. A haze of smoke hung in suspension above the inert cinema screen. In one corner he could see a mound of waterproofs and gumboots. In another corner a Civil Defence woman was sorting through a heap of clean clothes.

Harry looked up at the steep aisle steps that were flanked on either side by prostrate shapes, most smoking or resting under blankets. Few were talking, and he realised the rest centres were not geared towards the retelling of experiences; they were places for brief escape. He wondered if it was deliberate that the venues chosen were all places where, even during normal circumstances, it was impolite to talk.

At the front, to the right, bare trestle tables were arranged and manned by the blue-serge-uniformed Civil Defence staff and a number of volunteers in normal dresses and nylon aprons. Harry made his way over to the tables packed with food and drink. He saw two polished urns surrounded by assorted cups and mugs. Next to them were rows of cheese and ham sandwiches, pies, assorted biscuits and a leaning tower of paper plates. A woman approached him and touched his arm with concern.

"Do you need a cup of tea, love?" she asked.

Harry's mouth was so dry and his lips so cold that he merely nodded. He tugged himself out of his wet coat and sank down onto a cinema seat. She said that he should help himself to food. He knew it was the perfect time to launch into a conversation but he suddenly didn't feel well. She left to make his drink.

He felt a compulsion to press his hand to his chest and feel the violent hiccup of his heartbeat, but when he did so he could barely detect it. He moved his fingers between his collarbones and felt it stronger there. While checking his pulse, he listened to the women industriously giving an inventory of their remaining supplies. After the uniformed lady had given him the tea, he noticed she was covertly studying the female volunteer next to her. It was clear to him, as the Civil Defence lady fussed over the urns and the trays of food, that what she really wanted to fuss over was her aproned assistant, who was absorbed in cutting thin strips off a catering-sized brick of cheddar.

"The generosity of people, eh?" the lady in uniform whispered to her friend as she sliced. "We've got so much bread we don't know what to do with it. I hope that urn stays hot. Those are our own urns, not the cinema's. We've had problems with that urn leaking before. Let's have a few more slices of cheese and then we can start buttering."

The woman cutting the cheese moaned suddenly, dropped the knife and sucked her finger.

"Oh! Let's have a look. I'll get you a plaster."

"I'm fine," the woman said, but Harry could see what the Civil Defence lady had picked up on; the young woman, even while she answered appropriately, seemed disorientated.

"I've a plaster in my bag."

"Please don't bother yourself."

Harry was reminded of a confused but polite ghost.

"It's no bother at all."

The Civil Defence lady hurried out of sight and came back

waving a plaster. The young woman gave up protesting and presented her cut finger. It was only when the Civil Defence lady had finished putting the plaster on that she realised the woman in front of her was crying.

"Thanks," the woman said, pressing at her tears with a handkerchief and returning to the block of cheese.

"Love, stop a minute. Are you from Aberfan?"

Harry, one hand pressed hard to his fluttering heart as he reached for the cup of tea at his feet, continued to watch them curiously.

The young woman nodded grimly.

"Are your family okay?"

"My daughter. She's nine. My husband is digging. I've got to keep busy."

"They'll find her, love."

The woman nervously smoothed a lock of her hair in her left hand. It was a minute or two before she spoke.

"She didn't make it. My husband is helping to find her friends and classmates. Half the house is gone. I can't go home without him."

The Civil Defence lady embraced her tightly and then let her go.

"You keep busy. That's the best thing."

The woman from Aberfan began to cry again, but they both wiped away her tears. The Civil Defence lady gently pressed a butter knife into the mother's hand and placed a loaf and a tub of margarine in front of her. The older lady deftly opened the bread packet with a flourish that told of a thousand opened before and extracted half of the sliced loaf. The young mother in her apron, slightly reassured, took up buttering the bread as another flood of exhausted and filthy volunteers filed through the door.

Harry resolved to speak sympathetically to the mother. He could easily initiate a conversation by going up and saying that he had overhead the exchange. If she didn't want to talk to him, then that was fine. He rubbed his temples and realised he was sweating profusely. He took his pulse again and found that it was stuttering. He began to feel dizzy.

The Civil Defence lady noticed that Harry was bathed in a sheen of sweat and came over to ask how he was feeling. He tried to respond but all he could do was gulp for air.

"I'm getting Doctor Elliott," she said.

Moments later, a greying but confident man approaching fifty was bent down at the side of Harry's seat. In the narrow space, Harry pulled the next few cinema seats down with the help of the Civil Defence lady and put his feet up. The doctor asked him to undo a few shirt buttons and then listened to his chest with a stethoscope. Frowning, he took Harry's blood pressure and then undid the cuff.

"You're soaking." Dr Elliot said, and then asked the Civil Defence lady to find Harry something to change into.

"Am I having a heart attack?"

"Has this kind of thing ever happened before?"

"Never."

"When did you first start feeling ill?"

Harry explained he'd been feeling all right until he got to the rescue centre. He wasn't sure whether to mention the fact that he'd missed a deadline. While it was indicative to him that something was wrong, the doctor probably wouldn't understand the significance.

"When was the last time you ate or drank anything?"

"I don't think this is indigestion, doctor. I've had indigestion before and this isn't it."

"That's not why I asked. Did you eat anything at lunch?"

"I haven't had anything since breakfast. I had a couple of slices of toast and a cup of tea."

"Nothing since then?" The doctor looked at his watch. "So we're talking about ten hours ago?"

"They gave me the cup of tea when I arrived here."

"Do you smoke?"

Harry shook his head as he did up the buttons on his damp shirt. If anything could make him start smoking again, it was a day like this. The doctor put his stethoscope and blood pressure cuff back in his bag.

"Have you ever had any heart problems in the past?"

"No."

"Are you on any medication?"

"No."

"Allergic to anything?"

"No."

"Any pain travelling down your left arm?"

Harry confirmed he had no pain there.

"You say you had a pain in your chest. Can you describe the pain? For example, was it a crushing pain or a stabbing pain?"

"My chest felt tight and I couldn't breathe. I was having palpitations."

Harry found that talking to the doctor was reassuring in itself.

"Okay. I wouldn't worry about this being a heart attack or heart-related pain. I think we can safely put it down to the situation of the day. You're covered in muck; you've been walking around in the cold and the rain; you've eaten nothing. I would say you're just exhausted and overwhelmed. The sweating and tight sensation when breathing points to anxiety. Have you ever had an anxiety attack before?"

"No, but it has been overwhelming today, and I had a bit of a fall in the spill."

"Not surprising you fell. It's impossible to get around in. Your pulse is fast and your blood pressure is slightly raised, which is understandable given the circumstances. Our friend here will get you some hot chocolate after she's found you something to change into. I've got a few others to see and then I'll be back. If you feel like eating something, I think you should try."

Soon after the doctor had moved on, the Civil Defence lady

returned with a bundle under her arm. She ushered Harry in the direction of the cinema toilets, where he peeled off his shirt and jumper.

Shivering and weak, he folded his garments neatly, laid them to one side and pulled on a clean vest, a shirt that pulled at the buttons, and a coarse brown jumper. He felt comforted and more like his old self, albeit shaken. When he came back to his seat there was a hot chocolate and folded grey blanket waiting for him. He drank the hot chocolate quickly, wrapped the blanket around him, leaned his head back and closed his eyes. He had only been resting for a few minutes when a loud voice punctured his fragile peace.

"Do you mind if we take a couple of photographs?"

Clearly, he wasn't the only reporter who thought the rescue station a good place to interview witnesses. The change of mood in the cinema was tangible.

"And if anyone wants to talk, this is your opportunity to share your thoughts with the British nation. Who's to blame for this terrible disaster?"

A few dirty, dishevelled heads shot up and swore sharply. The London journalist – another of Falstone's sort – appraised the whole cinema candidly. When his gaze fell on the tearstained face of the woman making sandwiches, he did a double take and his eyes narrowed.

"Hey," he said walking and then half jogging towards her. "You're unsteady there. You look like you could use a sit down."

Confidently, the journalist squeezed his way through behind the trestle table, put an arm around her shoulders and guided her to a seat at the other end of Harry's row. Harry felt too weak to intervene without bringing on another attack. He couldn't remember the last time he had been so stressed.

"Where do you think you're going with her?" the Civil Defence lady said, standing in front of the journalist as the mother sat down and blinked at them both.

The London journalist scowled, then said: "Even an idiot

can see she's in shock. You've got her on her feet working? You ought to be ashamed."

"Well, I never!" said the older woman in uniform.

"But I was helping," the mother said to the journalist.

"You've been through a great deal, love. It's written all over you." The journalist patted the mother's hands and nodded for the photographer, watching, to get himself ready. "Take your time, love. When did you first notice something was wrong?"

"When did I first notice...? I... I was washing up the breakfast things. I always have to do things straightaway otherwise the scrambled egg gets stuck in the pan. I heard a noise..."

The journalist nodded and the volunteers drew near to listen.

"Like a big rumble of thunder..."

"I thought it was a jet engine," someone said in the background.

"I knew there wasn't something quite right, but... I don't know. I put the dishes away and pottered, but there was something about the loudness of that sound. I went outside and there was a boy running towards me. He was terrified and upset."

"Did you recognise him?" the journalist asked.

"It was Betty's boy, but I didn't know at first because he had this terrible gash on his head. His face was covered in blood. I tried to catch him – make him come to me so I could bandage his head – but he was too scared. He said he had to find his mother." The woman suddenly jumped up as if she'd forgotten something, her eyes filled with tears. "I should find him," she said in panic. "I must see if he got home."

The journalist guided her back to her seat with an expression of reassurance.

"But what about your own children?"

"I've only got one daughter – Nerys."

"Is Nerys okay?"

"No."

"She didn't make it?"

The woman buried her head in her hands and wept. The journalist gently pushed her hands down from her face and the photographer obliged him by taking the picture.

The sharp flash caused half the rescuers to bolt upright in their seats and gaze around in confusion. Harry did an intake of breath in shock.

"That's enough! Get out of here, you bloody parasites," the Civil Defence lady said, running and snatching up the butter knife, still covered with a thick smear of yellow margarine. "This may not be sharp enough to kill you, but I swear I'll do as much damage as I can."

She advanced towards the journalist. He didn't look the least bit intimidated, but the back of his collar was soon grabbed by one of the miners. Protesting, he and the photographer with him were removed from the auditorium and, Harry assumed, the cinema itself.

When Dr Elliott returned just under an hour later, Harry felt weak and embarrassed. The doctor had brought two cups of tea, one for himself and one for his patient, which they sipped side by side.

"I don't know if you take sugar, but I've put one spoon in yours. It'll do you good."

"Are you from Aberfan?" Harry asked.

"I'm an occupational health doctor with the NCB, so I'm attached to the rescue groups."

"I bet you've seen a few things," Harry said.

"Not today, I haven't. I haven't been outside this cinema since I got here."

"Is it all mining accidents with the NCB?"

"It's mostly the usual occupational health stuff – getting the miners back to work when they've been sick. But miners' rescue can be tough. How are you feeling?"

"Better."

"Not a heart attack?"

"No, thank goodness."

"It would get the best of anyone – a day like this. What brings you here, anyway?"

Harry couldn't avoid answering truthfully. "I'm a journalist."

"Not Fleet Street, though."

"How can you tell?"

"I'm not patching up your broken nose," Dr Elliott said, pointedly looking up at the rows of seats behind them. Harry responded with a wry smile.

Harry slept fitfully that night, at one point waking up in a cold sweat despite the blanket. He let out a sigh but masked it with an emotional cough. Burying his forehead in the crook of his elbow, he pressed against his eyes to stem the tears. His mind kept throwing up specific words as though he was incapable of more complex thought. Two words came to mind repeatedly: 'vulnerable' and 'love'. The first mostly applied to himself and to the victims of the disaster. He believed 'love' related to a wider context, or maybe the lack of it in his life. Pressing his eyes again, he rolled onto his side and faced the back of the cinema seat.

Before dawn, Harry left the latest arrival of exhausted volunteers in the cinema and made some notes in the foyer while sipping lukewarm coffee. He knew he looked terrible, that his hair was standing on end; he needed a shave and he felt ten years older. Days didn't get worse than the day before. The tearstained face of the young mother in the cinema, frozen in the blinding photographer's flash, was an image he could not shake off. For some journalists, days like the previous one were nothing more than a means of light entertainment.

Chapter 4

Fleet Street can stick its fake typewriter emotions up its arse, Harry thought, slapping *The Daily Telegraph* down on the newsdesk with the kind of savagery reserved for swatting summer flies.

Ten months had passed since the disaster, and while Harry frowned on any sort of cheap sensationalism, Fleet Street reporting of Aberfan was a complete anathema to him. He found it hard to believe the hardnosed national journalists were affected at all. Occasionally, he would try to give them the benefit of the doubt. What if the disaster had got to them as they embraced and walked among it, eagerly taking notes? It was possible they had lain sleepless and tormented in their booked-out beds at the Mackintosh Hotel. Perhaps, after they had returned to whatever part of England they came from, they had taken to drinking. Perhaps they had hugged their own children all the harder. Perhaps not, he concluded; they're a pack of animals.

Sometimes flashbacks would slam through his thoughts without warning, but recently he had begun to willingly recap on the events at Aberfan, wanting to ensure that his own experience, painful though it was, could not be polluted by the shameless crowing of his peers. He considered himself a first-hand witness. The tragedy was not to be used and exploited.

Huw, who was always to a greater or lesser degree florid-faced with rosacea, spread *The Telegraph* and leaned over the story. He scanned it and returned Harry's glare with diplomatic resignation.

"Are you really telling me," Huw said, "that if the *Daily Mail* or *Telegraph* offered you another go, then you wouldn't take the chance?"

"No, I bloody wouldn't!"

"How's your Bridget these days?"

"Fine, as always," Harry replied, noting Huw's deliberate change of subject.

People were leaving around them, sidestepping the papers which littered the floor as they did so. A bolt of sunlight suffused the thick pipe and tobacco smoke with a sallow flush. A couple of telephones, insistent and impatient, rang and rang.

Huw pulled on his houndstooth jacket, patted his pockets and nudged Harry's elbow for them to follow the exodus. In the street, Harry hurried ahead to distance himself and swallowed a hard breath, blinking in the daylight. The sun was high and gusty; he found the chill wind refreshing after the newsroom stuffiness. A new season was on the way and a new boss, Taylor, had arrived. An easterly wind brought the smell of Brains Brewery – a warm smell of bitter and boozy fermenting flowers – to Wood Street and Thomson House.

It was unusual to see so many reporting staff exiting the newsroom en masse. People passing might have assumed those leaving the building were responding to a fire alarm, and the journalists themselves accepted the evacuation in a similar vein. The scheduled meeting in a local pub was an enforced break and, as welcome as it was, it was still a little annoying. Grumbling accordingly, the motley group continued along the road, waked past the main Post Office and then crossed onto Golate lane. Even at that distance from Thomson House, the printing presses could still be heard. Evan, the editor of the *Echo*, his shirt more wrinkled than usual and his grey hair badly in need of a cut, hung at the back of the group with their new managing director.

There was plenty of room in the Queen's Vaults, a favourite of the journalists. The sudden increase in noise caused the few locals to turn their heads, frowning.

When everyone was settled, Evan introduced Mr Taylor.

"You may find it strange that I have organised a trip to the pub," Taylor said, getting to his feet. He was tall and loomed over his staff. "You might have expected me to address you in the boardroom, but I felt it important to meet you in the reporters' natural habitat." There were a few polite nods from the listening group. "I realise, of course, that you make your contacts in the public houses, and I'm happy to keep paying your expenses for you to do so – provided, of course, that you keep delivering stories which entertain our readers."

As Mr Taylor took a long, relaxed breath and stared for a moment at the ceiling, the group around him looked grim. Harry caught Evan's eye, nodded sharply and threw him a questioning look. Evan responded with a subtle shake of his head. Mr Taylor continued:

"We are going to adopt a new competitive outlook. Our rivals are not other local papers but actually Fleet Street, and we need to learn from them – their ways of working and the techniques they use. I have big ambitions—"

Harry stood up and proceeded to drink his fresh pint in one go as the group, including Mr Taylor, looked on in surprise. The managing director had ceased talking, but he continued to stand in the belief that the assuming and surly fellow to his left would realise his faux pas and sit down. Huw tugged at Harry's sleeve to get him to sit but only succeeded in causing Harry to slop some of his beer onto his hand. Harry thumped the glass down on the beermat, leaving half an inch rolling in the bottom.

"I have an ambition to finish what I was doing in the way I've always done it," he said.

Evan watched in astonishment as Harry left.

"Maybe his wife called him home again to make sure his tie is still straight and his shoes are still polished," George said. "She wants to put the iron away and start living."

"You'd do well to try smartening up yourself sometime!" Evan shot back. "A tie wouldn't hurt." He turned to the managing director. "Harry's got a lot on, Mr Taylor. I can only apologise. Please continue."

"I was about to hand over to you, anyway," Taylor said in a somewhat preoccupied fashion as he sat down again.

Evan rapped his lighter on the table. The group, distracted by concerns about their expenses, turned to him.

"And we have a new member of staff on the *Echo* team. This is Julian."

Julian stuck up a hand in a half wave. They'd seen the boy around the newsroom for about a week, but nobody had taken much notice. What did surprise them was when Evan explained that Julian was the new cub reporter. They'd all assumed copyboy or work experience, but looking at him now, there was something that set him apart from the usual recruits. A bright look in his eyes told them he was clever for his age.

"Are we dabbling in child labour?" George said. "They don't serve milkshakes here, kid."

"Julian's just graduated. He'll be working on the *Echo* team and he's Mr Taylor's nephew, although I'll say now that's nothing to do with him being taken on. He was hired on merit before Mr Taylor here had even accepted the job."

Mr Taylor nodded and brushed a thin black fringe from his forehead, careful to avoid eye contact with his relative.

"What's the deal with that Harry fellow?" Mr Taylor asked Evan when the staff were busy firing questions at the new recruit.

"Oh, he just likes to keep himself to himself, Mr Taylor, but he's won I don't know how many awards. Writes some fantastic copy, but... anyway, he's going to have to lighten up tonight. He's got this *Ulysses* story between his teeth. Harry is a big fan of the novel and there's a film adaptation out, directed by some fellow called Strick. Cardiff have banned the film and Harry is furious. Newport, on the other hand, licensed the film. I'm sending him there to watch the film and tell us what the fuss is about. I'm sending Julian with him."

Harry's impulse to race back to work had subsided as soon as he was outside the Queen's Vaults. He regretted having made a scene. The chance to size up any opposition to the new direction had been wasted. He stood uncertainly on the pavement and wondered how long his colleagues were going to be. When it became apparent they had no intention of leaving, his restless legs took him back to Thomson House. Journalism, he thought, was like Thomson House itself. From the outside, the building was deceptively simple: the latest in 1960s design, a neat rectangle with an additional overhang above reception to protect visitors from the rain. Inside, the reliable and old-fashioned ways persisted. It was a rabbit warren of small rooms – machine workshops messy with glue, fresh paper, screwdrivers, portable radios, and tea trays with white canteen china. Everything was linked by ill-lit, creaky corridors and squeezed around the great printing hall.

Standing outside Thomson House, throwing a glance over his shoulder to see if anyone had followed him, he was reminded of the *Echo* and *Western Mail*'s move from St Mary Street. The new building had been adorned in flags and bunting. Roy Thomson had promised that the staff would be drawn from the local community. Management and editorial, he had assured the happy crowd, would be drawn from their own people – the Welsh. Thomson wanted a staff with a sense of place. Thomson was faithful, Harry thought as he headed into the foyer. The last place Thomson thought about when it came to a sense of place was Fleet Street.

Chapter 5

The young couple kissing in the row in front hadn't noticed that the lights had gone up. A handful of individuals had sat alone in the front stalls, presumably hoping the film would be as titillating as the ban in Cardiff suggested. It was a slow night for the Odeon cinema on Clarence Place. For all of its American architecture – the ostentatious central fin and canopied curving entrance – there was nothing atypical about the inside. A cinema was a cinema, after all – the stale popcorn smell and the dusty red velvet seats, the carpet tacky with the dregs of sugary spilled drinks. Harry was aware that he and Julian could probably be mistaken for father and son. The rear stall tickets had been free – offered to the *Echo* when he made his enquiries.

Harry tried hard not to think about the last time he had been in a cinema, when he had been moved to tears. He thought about the boy instead, wishing he could help Julian out with the occasional bit of reference to Joyce's book. That would be more useful than teaching him about journalism. Harry wondered if he was underestimating him. Julian might well be running the paper itself in a year or two. Such cases weren't unheard of. He resolved to find out whether Julian was indeed just a beneficiary of nepotism. If the boy was, then Harry, with justification, could return to working alone.

Twice while watching *Ulysses*, Harry had gone to look at his watch and found that he needed to move his wrist around until light caught the hands in the celluloid gloom. The second time, he was forced to wait until Molly and Bloom were caressing each other on the cliff tops. The scene reminded him of a daytrip he had taken with Bridget to Flat Holm. It was a matter of pride to him that none of his colleagues realised she had left him years ago. He hated sympathy.

Later, in Ye Olde Murenger with Julian, Harry stretched in his seat at the back of the pub, glad of the space. In the cinema he had been forced to lean his weight to one side to avoid the boy's arm, which had hogged the joint armrest, something Harry deeply resented.

Harry had to hand it to Strick, the film director, because the man had managed to enrage Catholics and conservatives alike with the most pedestrian film in the history of cinema. Joyce's *Portrait of the Artist* was routinely taught in schools and it was mystifying that Harry's hometown of Cardiff had banned the film of *Ulysses*, necessitating a twelve-mile trip to Newport to see it play. What was wrong with people like Doxsey? Harry suspected that the Tory councillor with a hand in film licensing was corrupt. There was a network. And now Sidney Doxsey had accused the *South Wales Echo* of getting its staff to write into Postbag with the intent of whipping up feeling. The film wasn't that bad. You couldn't get the real flavour of Joyce, of course. It didn't translate the same. But the film was as faithful as it could be.

Harry watched as Julian, waiting for the pints to settle at the bar, drew on a cigarette and flicked through his notebook. Had Julian studied Joyce at whatever elite school he'd attended?

"So, what did you think of the film, Harry?"

"I see what Strick was trying to do."

"I found it rather dull, if I'm honest, right up until the last fifteen minutes. Molly, is it? Bloom's wife. She's interesting."

"Didn't you study Joyce in college?"

"No, we studied the Greats. Classics."

"Useful. Well, I didn't think the film was that bad. If they don't lift the ban, I'll move to bloody Newport."

"And work for the *Argus*?"

"Cheeky bastard."

"I wasn't saying it to be rude."

"Who wants to work for the *Argus*? I'll commute to Cardiff."

Julian regrouped and tried again: "What was the fuss at Cannes?"

"Strick pulled it himself," Harry said. "Some Frenchie had subbed his subtitles. I know that feeling – like subs hacking your story to death. He stopped the picture halfway through."

"So it's not just Doxsey against it, then?"

"The world is full of morons, but Doxsey is mine."

"Are you going to 'turn him over'?"

Harry noticed Julian's brief, unwitting smile and read in it the boy's enjoyment of sounding like a seasoned reporter.

"It's my new mission in life."

"For banning *Ulysses*?"

"Stress the second syllable," Harry said, contemplating for a moment.

"Pardon?"

"The second syllable. All your emphasis is on the first."

"YOOL-i-seez."

"Try again."

"YOOL-i-seez."

"Don't they teach you anything in college?"

"I went to YOO-niversity, Harry. All the stress is on the first syllable."

"Why journalism?" Harry asked.

When Julian told Harry about his love of writing, his scholarship to Oxford and how inspired he was by Fairlie's political column in *The Spectator*, Harry was surprised and encouraged.

"Well," Harry said, "you might do some good here. There's too much corruption in Cardiff. It's endemic. It's the councillors. Too many businesspeople getting involved with politics to further their own business interests. It's out of hand."

"That's why you're so interested in Doxsey?"

"I've been waiting for one of them to slip up for years. Before I retire, I'm going to expose one or all of the bastards. There are two kinds of corruption in Wales. There's Tory corruption like Doxsey: city stuff, planning backhanders and contracts to do with redevelopment. Then you've got the Valleys: Labour fiefdoms, like what you'll find in North East England, places like County Durham. Any council job, from park warden to head teacher, has to be gained by canvassing every councillor and alderman, pretending you've got the same hobbies, taking flowers for their wives and toffees for their kids. If you've got your eye on a particular council house in a particular area, you'd better vote Labour."

"Then why don't you do something? If you know so much about it...?"

"It's on such a universal scale. When it's done, it has to be done properly. A big enough splash to have them all scrambling to get out of the pool."

Harry curled his hands into fists, splayed them up as if in sudden surrender and then let them fall with a depressed smack onto the table.

"That woke me up," said Julian.

"I'm trying to rouse myself," Harry said, drawing out the vowels.

"For a fight?"

"Maybe later."

"Not with me, I hope."

Harry sat upright as though he'd remembered something, fumbled to his side and pulled out the *Echo*.

"I've got a couple of stories in, but I didn't have time to get to the office. Christ – these subs! It's only a down-page piece, but still, they ought to get it right. This your first story – this slum clearance?"

"What do you think of it? Not bad?"

"Topical. The writing's bloody filthy."

Julian took the paper and admired his own article as Harry

briefed him on the meeting they were about to have with Councillor Jones, the Chairman of the Newport Protection Committee, who was responsible for allowing the film to play in the city. Councillor Jones ran a successful construction company, so it wasn't as though Doxsey could accuse him of being some beatnik. Harry told Julian that he should lead the interview with the man; if Harry needed any further information, he would jump in towards the end. Julian opened his new notebook. Harry told him to write the date in it.

The councillor arrived and for a moment Julian was visibly shocked at the large size of the man's stomach and the way his round-shouldered frame accentuated the poor fit of his beige suit. When he sat down the jacket rode further up, as if trying to escape over his head. After the initial introductions were over, Harry left to fetch some drinks. Only as he was creeping back towards the table, trying not to spill anything, did Councillor Jones get around to the film.

"There are worse things on television." The councillor sipped his beer. "If we're talking about films, then personally I like cowboys and Indians. You can't beat it for entertainment and that's why I go. People should have a choice. It's out in paperback, for goodness' sake. Anyone can buy it if they've got a few bob."

"A good point," Julian said, committing his words to shorthand. "You've read it, Mr Jones? *Ulysses*?"

"Tried, more like. Heavy going."

"You've got to read *Portrait of the Artist* first. It doesn't make complete sense, otherwise." Julian smiled at Harry for giving him the tip.

Councillor Jones gave a shrug which was swallowed by his own jacket. If I'm not careful, Harry thought, that's what I'll look like in a year or two, and I'll have all those years of Brains and other bitters to blame.

Harry saw himself as a glass-half-full man, especially if it was half full of amber or black on a table of brown bottles and tankards. There wasn't anything to dislike about pubs: talk and tobacco, coats and caps, frosted glass and the inevitable dartboard illuminated by a spotlight like some gallery exhibit. Always there was a couple bickering who ended the night dancing together, fingers entwined, swaying against each other. Always there was some sad, toothless old-timer with braces and a cigarette hanging from his lips, bent at the knees and frowning in concentration as he twisted, alone, oblivious to whatever came on the jukebox.

"Do you find the ban hypocritical?" Julian said.

"I'm just saying there are more strip clubs in Cardiff than Newport. More prostitutes on the streets. It's more overt. Why bury a tame film? I was expecting something scandalous."

"And how do you decide whether you will allow a film or ban it?" Julian continued.

"We've got a good panel. Just about the right mix of different people. That's what you want. We've got a couple of intellectuals, a couple of women. We sat around, smoked some cigarettes and had a chat about public prejudice."

"Cardiff is alleging you only allowed the film because they had already banned it. What do you say about that? Tit for tat, so to speak? What's your response?"

Julian's gaze flicked to Harry, who had noticed that his question sounded a little rehearsed, as though the boy held ambitions to work in television.

"Oh," the councillor said, "I'm sure they'd like to think that every decision we make is influenced by them, but we've got our own minds. When it screened in America first, I expected a few complaints, but actually, the American Catholics were okay about it. I suspect there's a lot of that going on – people getting wound up about the hype. Once they see it, it's pretty tame."

"Anyone over here complain?"

"Like I said, I expected lots of letters, but I only had one."

"What do you think people make of the film?"

"To be honest, because of the fuss made by places like Cardiff, the film gets hype it doesn't deserve."

For the first time, Julian looked to Harry to help him out. Harry might have been an old journalist, but he hadn't forgotten that taking notes while having a conversation and really concentrating could be tiring at first. He sensed Julian's attention slipping. And it was late. The councillor looked tired, too.

"I agree. It's not a patch on the book," Harry concluded. "Joyce's genius is in the language, of course."

"When will you boys be running it?" the councillor asked.

"Tomorrow. Julian's only just started with us. He's lucky. My first month, I had nothing but obituaries and market vegetable prices."

"I'd better be off, if you've got everything," the councillor said, and the bell rang for last orders.

Once the councillor had left, Julian turned to Harry.

"How do you think it went?" the boy asked.

"It's something, anyway." Harry wondered whether to be critical or kind. "Went well. You've got enough for the story. You've got a bit of conflict with his nice response to Cardiff's accusation of tit for tat. The real test, of course, is what it's like when you've written it up."

"How long have you been doing this?"

"You're interviewing me now?"

"Are you in a rush? Tell me about your best time. What's the highlight?"

Not working with you, Harry thought, but instead said: "My best time? You talk as if I'm retired."

"I meant what's the highlight so far? The awards?

"Fleet Street, I guess. While it lasted."

"Did you learn a great deal?"

"My pal – showing me the ropes – taught me his way of doing a story. If it was a conflict piece where someone did something bad to someone else, I'd phone the good guy in the morning. Then we'd get a bit wasted in the pub. Couple of hours later I'd return to the office ready for a fight. I'd phone the bad guy in the afternoon and keep my fingers crossed that he'd tell me to fuck off. Then I'd put that in the story."

"How did you end up in Cardiff?"

"That's another story."

"What happened?"

"Monumental cock-up. I'll tell you another time."

Harry leaned forward with his elbows on his knees and stared grimly at the garish carpet. The barman interrupted their silence to remind them it was last orders and then took their empties to the bar. Glasses clinked as he weaved among the tables collecting the ashtrays and empties. Two drunks noisily bid goodnight to each other.

"Come on, Harry."

"You can't possibly be interested."

"I'm waiting."

"The guy I mentioned started getting to the pub earlier and earlier. I'd join him over lunch. I'd have four pints myself. I didn't get in the Mucky Duck – that was our favourite pub – until after one. My friend could barely stand by then. Said he'd been hauled in by top brass. Then he keeled over. I took him home and raced back to Fleet Street. He'd been doing this story about a rabid – literally rabid – dog that had been found in Surrey. The police were spooked, held off using their own dogs for a bit. Didn't want their police dogs foaming at the mouth. So I wrote it up. Schoolboy error. They sacked him and me on the same day. Said they only wanted writers who write their own stuff. The *Echo* threw me a bone."

"That's awful."

"Is it?"

Julian stared at Harry.

"You wouldn't say that if you'd been at Aberfan. I was one of the first journalists to arrive. Now that *was* awful."

39

Chapter 6

"Alcatraz?" Evan repeated.

"Exactly."

Harry had discovered that Alderman F G Davies was going to ask Parliament whether the council could relocate Cardiff Prison. The newsdesk thought the story sounded like a good page lead, especially if they could have a bit of fun with proposed locations, which included Flat Holm Island.

"Let's make it a feature," Evan said. "Get the stats on the real Alcatraz. What're the chances of it really happening?"

"None at all," Harry replied, "but the readers will enjoy it. No one would get near the bloody place in winter. We should be humanising the penal system, not the other way around. It'll be worse than Dartmoor."

Truth was that Harry maintained a fondness for the island since his trip there with Bridget, bad weather or not. She had been slim at the time, charming and full of character. Taking a boat trip seemed romantic, though they were forced to wait an age for it to arrive. As the gulls circled and cried, a ray of sunlight had hit the water between them and the island, giving it the appearance of levitating on a silver band. When the sun burst free, the sea glittered as though a boat carrying a thousand foil strips had sunk, sending its cargo to the surface. The salt wind and dazzling light made his eyes water. He looked away and knew in that moment that he was going to ask Bridget to be his wife. They would have a family. Harry treasured the memory for its innocence.

"There's always Steep Holm, if they want to expand," Evan said, breaking in on his thoughts. "The guards could row between the two."

"Yeah, they could. Though they'll be permanently covered in bird shit."

What Harry liked most about his job was having a mind full of workable stories which blotted out too much thinking.

Alderman Davies, the brains behind the prison move, met Harry in the City Arms at midday. Harry went for one of the stronger ales and promised himself he'd stick to two pints. Davies said the project didn't look like it would get off the ground. The former Minister of State at the Home Office, Jellicoe, had given Davies his personal assurance that if – and only if – the council could find somewhere suitable to relocate the prison, then they'd consider it. But Jellicoe had left suddenly and been replaced by Lord Derwent, and it was impossible to get hold of the new Minister.

Once they'd exhausted Flat Holm, Harry asked the Alderman whether he knew of Doxsey. Davies knew him, so to speak, but not well. Davies' sister lived round the corner from the Tory councillor. It was a nice road, he said, but Harry wasn't interested at all in what Doxsey's front garden looked like.

When the meeting was over, Harry used the pub phone to give Cardiff Prison a call. The head of the prison snorted on the line and said they'd just finished a programme of extension. He then hung up. On a whim, Harry placed a second call to Doxsey at his finance firm, Laurentide. Harry waved his hand to catch the barman's eye and motioned for him to bring another pint – taking his total to three. More than he'd promised. Barely able to hear the receptionist, he waved at the barman again, this time to keep the noise down. The barman curtsied with a low, comically old-fashioned bow. Harry could hear the receptionist whispering to someone else.

"Hello?" Harry said, with growing impatience. "Councillor Doxsey?"

"Yes. How can I help you?"

Harry introduced himself before explaining his role at the

Echo and his interest in Doxsey's decision to ban *Ulysses* in Cardiff. He then asked the councillor for an interview. There was a pause at Doxsey's end.

"Is that all?" he said, eventually.

"Yes. Our readers are interested as to why it's banned in Cardiff but they can still see it in Newport."

"I can fit you in at three in the afternoon, if it's not going to take too long."

Harry took Julian along to his appointment with Doxsey. Laurentide Securities was conveniently just around the corner from Thomson House. It was experience for Julian and he didn't want the boy using his desk or being asked to write copy in his absence. They were greeted by a tearful receptionist who appeared to be attempting to pull herself together one minute – reapplying a touch of mascara in a hand mirror or patting her hair – and then, chin trembling, mumbling tearfully to herself the next. The reception itself was every bit as depressed as the receptionist: hard wooden chairs, a dehydrated spider plant and a couple of folded, out-of-date magazines in the waiting area. After a short period, Mr Doxsey came out of the door to the left of the receptionist's desk.

"He'll have to wait in reception," Doxsey said, pointing at Julian.

"Why?" Harry said, no intention of actually bringing the boy in.

"Because there's no need for two of you. And do take no notice of her," he said, nodding at the receptionist.

"Fine." Harry turned to Julian. "Stay here."

Jaw clenched, the boy sat back down.

In a bright office with the sound of the traffic below drifting through the open window and the blinds knocking against the sill, Doxsey poured himself and Harry tea and offered an uninspiring choice of biscuits. There was something of Goody Two-Shoes about the neatness of Doxsey: the angular glasses sitting on his round nose on his perfectly round face and the prim way he took tea. There was also something annoying about the way he leaned forward and cocked his head to the side when talking. He reminded Harry of a boy he'd known in school, a lad with a singular talent of ratting on other boys. When Harry probed into Doxsey's past, he was not surprised to hear that Doxsey had been a used-car salesman. The problem of receptionists appeared to be at the forefront of his mind:

"I've had seventeen of them: seventeen bloody receptionists in two years. None of them any good. I try them out on low wages first – see if they're worth it before they start getting greedy."

"What exactly do you do here?"

"Finance. Businesses mostly."

"Right. So, this film. Have you read any Joyce?" Harry asked.

"No, I haven't. That okay, Shakespeare?"

"I think you've gone a bit overboard."

Doxsey blew out his cheeks in three quick puffs.

"It's blasphemous. The Catholic Church would be in uproar."

"Newport thought the same thing. They only had one letter. And the American Catholics allowed it."

"This isn't America, thank God. The film doesn't make sense and I don't believe the book does, either."

"Thought you said you hadn't read it?"

"You don't need to be a genius to work out it's rubbish."

"I'm of the opinion that it *is* genius. You read newspapers, Mr Doxsey?"

"Yes. Even yours. Sometimes."

"And does every news story in a daily have a connection to every other story in the paper? Probably not, besides the date."

"What is your point?"

"*Ulysses* is like the in-depth news of two ordinary characters on the same date, the sixteenth of June, who come together at the end. It's genius. And this is a university town, where students study English Literature. You've denied them that."

"Sounds like rot to me. If I had a son studying English Literature at Cardiff, I would be most displeased if he were to watch that film," Doxsey said.

"It's unnecessary censorship."

"You're entitled to your opinion."

"As is every other cinemagoer in Cardiff," Harry said, getting up.

On the way back to the office, Julian laughed about the fact that he had heard Harry arguing with Doxsey through the office door.

"I didn't realise I was that loud."

"You cheered the receptionist up, at least."

"I hope you weren't chatting her up."

"I've got a girlfriend. Actually, she was chatting me up, I think."

"You're not sure?"

"She had all these poems taped to her reception desk. You know the thing. Love lost, love gained. Full of sentimental longing – all that jazz. She asked me behind the counter to read them."

"I bet she did."

"I didn't really know what to make of it, but then she had this odd telephone call. I asked her about it afterwards. A female Tory colleague of Mr Doxsey is calling all the time, but he won't take her calls. The receptionist said this woman has threatened to involve the police before now. I wrote her name down. Mary something."

"Nothing would surprise me. Maybe I was a bit loud, but it was deliberate. That jumped-up car salesman back there doesn't want to protect people from smut. I'm going to expose the corruption in Cardiff, and when I do I'll see to it that they all get six to eight years in Flat Holm Prison."

"But there isn't a prison on Flat Holm."

"No. There isn't."

Chapter 7

"Should we even publish this? It makes me very uncomfortable," Harry said, handing back two letters to Evan after examining the notepaper front and back.

"What's the problem?"

"I'll write a piece about it if I absolutely have to, but I don't want to see the actual letters in the paper."

"Some bereaved mother in Aberfan is sending poison pen letters to other mothers with surviving children? That's pretty nasty stuff, Harry. Get the piece written and I'll think about the letters. And do try to be objective. I think it might be best if you give the police in Merthyr a call to check what they actually need."

"I just don't see the point in sticking it to some woman who's clearly ill. What if someone recognises her writing and takes matters into their own hands?"

"Maybe if we publish them she'll think twice and get some proper help? This is public interest first and foremost. The recipient's heartbroken. Her son was the only one in his class to survive – and now this."

"Bloody hell."

"I know. Kid had a pain in his side and his mother took him to the doctor."

Evan watched as Harry walked to the window, brooding. Harry couldn't help but imagine the writer of the letters watching bleakly from her own window as the surviving children walked to school with their mothers. He saw the child's bedroom turned into a museum collection. Toys were toys no longer but forensic reminders to unlock memory. Dolls, prams, toy cookers and dustpans, packs of playing cards, tin soldiers and wooden trainsets were now specifically not to be moved or altered. Not that Harry defended the poison penmanship, but he did feel there had to be a modicum of compassion. It was a minute or two before he spoke again:

"There's another danger here if we publish these letters. The Nationals could pick it up and start a witch-hunt. Let's not forget that someone is muckraking up there. Someone is deliberately trying to create stories."

"Who?"

"I don't know, but I'm going to find out. Someone is milking the tragedy. I'll do a little down-page piece about it."

Harry paused. It occurred to him that his desire not to publish the letters was as much about not giving the press ammunition as it was about his compassion for the sick woman.

"Everything okay, Harry?"

"Fine, of course. Why?"

"No reason," Evan said. "Take care of the poison pen letters after you've spoken to the police. If they're fine with it, I won't publish the letters themselves, but on the condition that you and Julian get cracking on the Aberfan report."

"Julian and I?"

"Yes."

"You cannot put a kid with no experience on this."

"There's too much for one person and you can oversee him. He's got a different style and I want to see what he can come up with. Harry, you're still on the splash. There's also a rumour that two senior officials from the NCB were in some kind of verbal altercation before the disaster which possibly distracted them from their jobs. And we can do something on the delivery of the report. You might want to get yourself to the Gas Board to see what the reaction is when the report goes on sale. Divide it as you see fit, Harry. You're in charge."

"The fuck I am, clearly."

"What else are you working on?"

"I think there's more to Doxsey than I first thought."

While Evan and Harry were discussing Doxsey, Julian was being told by the newsdesk to get another story on slum clearance. Five families were refusing to vacate their condemned homes in Newtown, the six overpopulated streets housing what was left of Cardiff's Irish community. He was also asked to put together a second story about the emotional and financial cost of demolition. The city was being dragged, sometimes kicking and screaming, into modernity. Before Julian left to take care of the jobs, Harry came out and told him that since the attention of Welsh people had been diverted to the National Coal Board's exploitation of them, it was possible they were blind to the serious exploitation closer to home.

Chapter 8

"Facts," said Harry, interrupting Julian the following day. "That's all anyone's interested in. There's a lesson for you. Feelings are for novels."

As the boy started to drone on about how useful he could be, Harry had a feeling there was something Julian had picked up in Doxsey's reception that might actually be helpful. Evan entered the newsroom and saw Julian appealing to Harry. Their editor marched towards them.

"He wants to stay on Doxsey," Evan said, watching as Julian made himself scarce. "He's only been here five minutes. Apparently, he's deeply concerned that he doesn't fall into the trap of writing about slum clearance. I think George has been winding him up. He was waiting outside my office when I arrived."

"What did you say to him?"

"I told him not to take any notice of people teasing him and that he can write a thousand words on the subject of damp houses. He's not a happy boy. Take him to the pub or something, would you? Take him under your wing. I don't want him in my office bothering me all day."

"But it's okay for him to bother me all day?" Harry said, taking Julian's jacket from the back of his chair and going to find the young reporter.

Outside, the pavements were chequered with damp. It was chilly in the shade but warm in the sun, which still had a little of the strength of summer left in it. The leaves were green, but there was a discernible change; they were drier, and this dryness made the wind sound stronger than it was; the leaves bent like meadow grass and, when the wind eased, they drooped altogether as though exhausted. Autumn would sweep the trees in a matter of weeks.

Harry and Julian headed for the Model Inn.

"Try this," Harry said, putting down two pints of strong black porter as Julian took in the nautical decor. They chatted about writing first, then Harry went for it: "What was the problem this morning?"

"Evan's not interested in my background."

"You're not old enough to have a background, are you? Anyway, editors aren't interested in backgrounds. You think Evan keeps track of every paper we've written at or every story we've done?"

"How am I going to stand out if I'm writing about Riverside clearance? I don't want to be 'slum guy'. It's hard talking to these people. In Newtown, no one would talk to me until the priest came along. When he asked me what I was up to, he virtually dragged people out of their houses. I could hardly look them in the eye."

"Ah, I know the Father. Transport Workers' Union official from Dublin. Ex-boxer. Very left wing."

"That's not the point."

"If you want to get ahead, you have to show it in your copy. Impress Evan; don't take up his time by whining."

"I only asked him if I could stay with the Doxsey story as well."

Harry's advice was that Julian hand in the thousand words of 'Is Your House Damp?' and do his best to make it the stuff of literary genius. Julian had been to Oxford, for goodness' sake. Surely he could make poetry out of moist air, burst pipes, damp patches and dry rot. And for those less au fait with damp proof poetry, he could include a list of the main causes of dampness at the side of the beautifully crafted article. Harry, noting Julian's mood lift, found his own spirits rising. The boy appreciated his advice.

"So, apart from James Joyce," Julian asked, "what else do you like reading?"

"Nothing."

"But I thought you liked literature?"

"What on earth gave you that idea?"

"You like Joyce."

"James Joyce is the only writer for me. Understand? I'm anti-intellectual, if you must know."

"Oh."

"I read Joyce because my grandfather lived in Eccles Street," Harry said, delighted with his preposterous lie. "That's the only reason."

Throughout most of the remaining afternoon, Julian kept out of Harry's business and worked furiously on his article. Time and again he leant over his typewriter, examining the text and then burying his hands in his hair as he cursed over the numerous typos. If Harry had felt any empathy, he might have shared the pork pie and Scotch egg that he'd picked up for lunch. Abstractly, he brushed the crumbs from his trousers. Once Julian had produced his legible and error-free copy, he handed it to Harry.

"In the subs' tray," he said, without looking at the offered papers.

Julian was subdued as he placed his masterpiece in the tray. Later, the newsdesk called Harry over to say that Julian's piece would be held for a sensational story about the gangster killing of John Buggy. I'll give him the bad news tomorrow, Harry thought.

Chapter 9

The next morning, if the presses had been silent, Julian would have been able to hear Evan bellowing Harry's name as he walked up the backstairs. As it happened, when he noticed the first edition rolling off, he took a second to watch the blur and roar. Upstairs, the yelling continued.

"Harry, get in here!"

All of the staff on the floor looked in the direction of Harry's desk. It was nothing unusual for Evan to shout, but Harry did not appear to be half as bothered as he should have been.

"What?" Harry said, more to himself, as if his attention was being pulled from something fascinating. In the end, he gave in and went to find out what Evan was so mad about.

Evan waved him into his office and slammed the door. The editor flopped down into his seat as though exhausted and stared at his reporter.

"I thought you were going to phone the police in Merthyr?"

"I gave them a call. They said they'd call back. They didn't. I had a deadline."

"They expected the poison pen letters to be published. Did you know that? Did you know they wanted extracts published?"

"If they'd have returned my call, I would have."

"They asked if we could run a bigger story today, with extracts of the actual letters and images. They're hoping someone recognises the handwriting."

Harry and his editor stared at each other.

"Your only saving grace, Harry, is that the police do want it handled sensitively. They'll treat any information from the public in the strictest confidence."

"Okay. I'll sort it out. Is that all?"

"No. Mr Taylor is coming in."

"What? What for?"

"He wants to know about your background with Aberfan."

"Why?"

"I don't bloody know. Just interested, I suppose. He's on his way down."

Harry rose to wait in the doorway. He was asked to grab an extra chair for Mr Taylor, but when the managing director arrived, he insisted on getting it himself.

"I hope you don't mind my taking up a little of your time?"

Harry shrugged. In the small room, the managing director was uncomfortably close.

"Aberfan's a big story and I didn't want to miss an opportunity to talk to our most distinguished reporter. Your work is very good."

"Thank you."

"Lots of awards, I hear."

"A few."

"There's quite a workload with Aberfan. Do you need any help?"

"No. Thank you. Evan did recommend Julian work on it with me, but he's busy on *Ulysses*."

Harry was relieved that Julian's ambition had been limited to working on a smaller story, but he was unsettled by the level of attention being directed at himself.

"*Ulysses*?" Mr Taylor said.

"Councillor Doxsey. We're going to turn him over."

"I'm not following," Mr Taylor said, turning to Evan with a look of good-humoured confusion.

"Councillor Doxsey banned the film *Ulysses* from showing in Cardiff," explained Evan. "Julian and Harry were writing about the fact that Newport didn't censor the film. Harry is a big James Joyce fan."

"Stress on the second syllable."

"What?" Evan said.

"Yoo-LI-seez."

"Give it a rest, Harry! For God's sake."

"Maybe Aberfan is a bit of an ask for a fledgling reporter. Can you give me some of the background?" Mr Taylor asked. "I read about it at the time, of course, but with so much going on... and who better than our chief reporter – one of the first of our boys on the scene?"

"Sure, Harry will fill you in," Evan said.

"Do you know the area, Mr Taylor?"

"Not at all."

Harry nodded and tapped a fresh cigarette from his packet, taking his time to light it.

"You're smoking again?" Evan said.

Harry shrugged away the question, cleared his throat, and then began:

"The borough of Merthyr is Y-shaped. The A470 and the A4054 form the branches of the Y. On the map, the River Taff forms the long straight line of the Y and a number of villages run along each side. Aberfan and Merthyr are on opposite sides of the river. I've seen aerial photographs since. The seven coal tips above Aberfan sat to the west of the canal – up the mountain. Tips five, six and seven overlapped each other slightly. From the air, they're like big, black teardrops running into one another."

Harry paused and looked at Evan, who nodded for him to continue.

"They said a tip had slipped – but there was no sense of the size of the disaster and I didn't realise anyone had been injured or killed. Everything seemed to be silent. Slowed down. Crowds were surrounding the school – digging. Horrific. Completely horrific. A lot of rescuers were desperate, using their hands until they had no skin on their fingers. There was water and slush and filth everywhere. The place was devoid of colour, completely monochrome – like being inside an *Echo* photograph or BBC newsreel; made me think of the screen we use to reproduce our pictures. There was a natural spring under the tips. This spring... caused one of the big black tears to roll down the mountain."

Harry sighed and looked out the window.

"But it sounds to me, from what I've heard, that you were buried yourself, in a way, by the London press," Mr Taylor said.

"He's normally a great journalist, Mr Taylor, but he did himself no favours."

"Where's this coming from? I don't know how you ran the *Dublin Evening News*, Mr Taylor, but I don't think you'd have believed it. They were ruthless."

"One or two bad apples, maybe—"

"More than one or two, Mr Taylor. A friend of mine, a social worker, told me the first thing she told people when she knocked on their doors was 'I'm not from the press or the Coal Board!' The press came first in that sentence."

"Evan said you used to work for Fleet Street yourself?"

"For a time."

"Why did you return to South Wales?"

"I needed a change. I prefer local to the Nationals."

"Strange. Most journalists would kill to work in Fleet Street."

"Would they?" Harry said without feeling.

"Look," Evan said, "I'd be annoyed myself, Harry. Wales is your turf and the big boys came down from London. But since you came back from Aberfan with next to nothing, you've been trying to prove yourself. I'm concerned you're pushing yourself too hard."

"What is this really about?"

"The Aberfan report is due in a couple of days. It's a huge amount of work. It's going to have all the evidence from the Tribunal. You'll finally have answers to those four questions. What happened? Why did it happen? Need it have happened? What lessons can we learn? I know you've been waiting months for it, but it might be too much. You've got any number of stories in the pipeline. You can't do it all. What do you think, Mr Taylor?"

"I think Evan is right, Harry."

"You know what I can't get my head around?"

The managing director and editor waited.

"I can't get my head around the fact that it happened at quarter past nine. Half an hour earlier, or a day later..."

Surprised at the conversational change in tack, Mr Taylor nodded and sighed.

"Do you have any kids yourself, Harry?"

Harry turned abruptly to face the managing director.

"No," he said, after a pause.

Evan and Mr Taylor glanced at each other.

"Work with Julian on Doxsey and at least consider allowing him to assist you on Aberfan. It'll take some of the pressure off," Mr Taylor said, and then stood and shook hands with Harry before striding mechanically out of Evan's office.

"What's it got to do with him?"

"He's a good guy. Worked on *The Sunday Times* for a bit. Anyway, if you're working together, then we'll have to get Julian set up with a desk. He's got nowhere to focus properly at the moment. Come on."

As Harry unhappily followed Evan back to his own desk, he brooded on how he hated types like Taylor. Guys like that came over as friendly, like with the enquiry about Aberfan, but underneath it all they were just businessmen. Evan stood at Harry's desk and Julian crept up behind them.

"Tidy up, for God's sake," Evan said to Harry.

"I need more room."

There were stacks of newspapers and folders. Harry's black and gold Remington typewriter was hidden among mounds of paper: old editions, journals, telephone directories and reference books. On the wall behind Harry's desk were clippings from the disaster. Evan tutted as he rescued two trophies from a box on the floor. Julian looked in the box and saw five or six other similar trophies. He could only see the dates on two: 1963 and 1964. Evan explained to Julian that Harry had won the Local Journalist of the Year Award for three years running.

"You should put these where people can see them," Evan said.

"If I put them where people can see them, would you put him somewhere else?"

"No. You're working together, Harry. You need to sit near each other."

"Well, put him over there!"

"You want me to put an *Echo* reporter on the *Western Mail* section?"

"True. There's no telling the bad habits he'd pick up."

"For Christ's sake, Harry. You sort it out. I've got better things to do."

Evan stalked off and Harry settled in his chair and ignored Julian, who sat facing a stack of Harry's dusty papers and locked his hands around his right knee. Harry looked at his clippings and then out the window, lost in racing recollections about the disaster: the sermons, the sandbags, the sandwiches, the distraught mothers and fathers, the pen-pushers and the good Samaritans.

"I might have something on Doxsey for you," Julian interrupted.

Harry blinked and frowned.

"You've only been here five minutes."

"Just a hunch I've got. About that telephone call..."

"A hunch."

Harry, without further comment, headed to the newsdesk. He interpreted the 'hunch' as no more than Julian's desperate and immature desire to impress. It was frustrating that he had shared his ambition with someone who was so naïve about Cardiff politics. He wished the boy would take his time and learn by watching and listening. It was a complicated business and not something to be rushed headlong into. Harry had yet to pin anything substantial on these men and it was a little impertinent of Julian to think it would be the easiest thing in the world. Julian's lack of patience could prove to be a hindrance rather than a help. Harry decided he would have to remind Julian of his place in the nicest way possible.

Harry had only sought the company of Huw on the newsdesk to escape his young colleague, but they had something for him. Huw handed him a story and a complaint letter that had been delivered to the *Echo* a couple of weeks prior. He saw the funny side at first, but the more he thought about it, the more serious he became. The Welsh National Angling Championships had been ruined by the vast amount of debris and discoloured silt in the River Taff. Harry placed a call to the Glamorgan River Authority who acknowledged within seconds there was a significant problem. The speed of their agreement made Harry curious.

"What's going on? Give me an update," he said.

"How long have you got?" said the man on the phone.

"Tell me."

"The Taff, from its source to Merthyr Tydfil, is suitable for drinking and the fish are healthy."

"The story starts well," Harry said.

"It does, but past Merthyr, it gets murky. The sewer at Treharris has been defective a few times, causing untreated cyanide waste to get into the river. It's killed the fish three times. The Treharris Anglers had a good case against the council, but they were put off after being told it would take years."

"Cyanide?"

"Hard to believe, right? The Taff then flows past the Hoover factory in Pentrebach. They've got their own treatment plant. They're clean, but the river is heading for coal mining areas, like Merthyr and Aberfan. The Aberfan disaster occurred partly because of a change in the type of coal sought after."

"You mean fine coal?"

"You know what I'm talking about. The tips used to be more stable when they were formed of larger lumps of coal. But then the NCB moved to fine coal and the tips were made up of a material rather like black sand. The NCB needs to stabilise these tips to prevent another tip disaster. That means washing away the top layers of fine particles, but the effect of this is that it gets into the river – hence the colour of the Taff."

"Is it all bad news?"

"There are still plenty of fish as far as Quakers Yard."

"And after?"

"There are no fish to Abercynon."

"What happens to the fish?"

"The Abercynon sewage farm is almost ninety years old. It overflows even during dry conditions. What with the surrounding industry removing coal by-products, the river is often poisoned with ammonia. Ammonia is bad news for fish."

"It's a bloody health hazard!"

"Yes. To Pontypridd, the Taff is a health hazard."

"And what happens after?"

"The two Rhondda rivers, choked with coal dust from old colliery spoils, join the Taff."

"This is disgusting," Harry said.

"Oh, you've heard nothing yet," the man replied. "The Treforest Industrial Estate has one rogue factory which doesn't take a blind bit of notice of anything we say. Every day, they discharge quantities of organic waste that would match the whole of Swansea's. It's too much for the north outflow and so pollutes the Taff down to Cardiff."

"You must do something," Harry said.

"We're trying. Where the NCB is concerned, they're not legally responsible for contamination from abandoned mines. With working collieries, since Aberfan, the priority has been safety. Tips have to be stabilised whether it pollutes the rivers or not. On the local level, the factory on the Treforest Industrial

Estate, for example, appealed to a minister after they got served notices under the Pollution Prevention Act. They won their appeal last month. The Minister decided that the best solution was not to penalise the factory but to improve sewerage systems."

"Which will take forever," Harry said.

"We've put prevention inspectors in place to monitor the river around the clock."

Harry concluded the call and couldn't understand why he hadn't put two and two together. Just like the corruption in Cardiff, the pollution was a complex intermingling of local and national wrongdoing. After lunch, Harry called the National Coal Board and gave them hell. They had the cheek to say that fishing in the Taff had improved, to which Harry replied that it may have improved in as much as some of the fish were still alive, but the person on the phone should explain that to the anglers whose lines brought up fairly indescribable catches.

"The fish would probably be relieved to be caught," Harry said.

He read a letter from one of the anglers which had already been published in Postbag. He resolved to write a page lead and let the NCB have just one line. He would leave it to the readers to comment.

Harry realised that only a couple of weeks ago, on a cloudy but bright day, walking along the left bank of the Taff and looking at the water, it had occurred to him that the white clouds reflected in the inky river like moonlight. At the time he considered it curious but thought no more of it. His mind had been busy elsewhere.

He had always found something calming about water. On his stressful days at work, with deadlines looming and people not getting back to him, he would take a five-minute breather and walk along the banks of the Taff. Yet despite his love for water, he had never taken to swimming. As a boy, he had attacked the lanes in the baths with force but swam no faster for it. Around once a year, usually when he was trying to improve his fitness, he would visit the Empire Pool, become completely exhausted after ten minutes, and then give up. He would hang on the side of the pool moving with the lapping of the water and wonder why immersion itself wasn't half as enjoyable as thoughts of it. It dawned on him eventually that it was natural water he was drawn to. Seas, rivers, streams, ponds and wells seemed to help him think.

He felt that the state of the Taff was a serious indictment of the state of the nation. They were polluted. They were exploited. They were poisoned. Harry thought of Aberfan and was reminded of some words from a service broadcast aired during the disaster that had stayed with him. Dr Glyn Simon had read from the Book of Isaiah: 'When you pass through the waters I will be with you; and through the rivers, they shall not overwhelm you'. Harry considered that if anyone did pass through the waters of the Taff, God himself might not be able to assist.

Chapter 10

Harry delighted at the titles. 'How to Undress in Public'. X-rated. 'The Magnificent Cuckold'. X-rated. 'Young Aphrodites'. X-rated. An advertised play caught his eye, too: 'The Killing of Sister George'. A controversial and notorious play about lesbians – performed in Cardiff. It had certainly been worth annoying the librarian for. There were some wonderful alternatives to *Ulysses* showing on the same night Doxsey and his friends made their fateful decision to ban the film.

Since Julian was working on another story, Harry decided to start putting the one about the film ban together. He thought it might lull Doxsey into a false sense of security until Harry found something – anything – on the councillor. 'Cardiff is the capital city', he typed, building up his words per minute, 'a prosperous and cultured university town. The whole thing casts Cardiff in a poor light'.

Something nagged Harry and he stopped typing. He leant forward and examined the story so far. What was missing? Yes. Councillor Davies had mentioned strippers. A phone call to the manager of the Tropicana nightclub confirmed that they had shown a strip act called Striparama during the week of the ban. You could see Striparama on the night the Licensing Committee had met, but not *Ulysses*.

Harry wondered whether it was worth the effort of finding out if any Cardiff University students were studying Joyce, but he dismissed the idea. They would probably be too academic and he had a deadline.

With the morning drawing on, Harry looked into the background of Strick, the film's director. There, too, was fresh information he could add to his story. Strick was a lifelong student of Joyce. The actors and actresses were professional.

The more Harry wrote, the more outrageous the ban seemed. It must have significance to Doxsey, thought Harry, as he attacked the keys on his typewriter. His working contentment calmed him and he found himself reconsidering the suggestion that Julian shadow him. Perhaps Julian could take on more of the grunt work, but he would make no decision yet.

When Harry finished typing out his story, he yanked the sheets from the spool and placed them in the subs' tray. It's people like Doxsey, he thought, who cause all the problems.

"You must have been in early," Evan said, noting the story in the tray.

"I've written that piece on *Ulysses*."

"Wasn't Julian—"

"Just the film ban. I've gone for a 'We're the Cultural Capital of Wales' feel. See what you think."

Harry leaned his chin on his hand and sighed over his typewriter. He was tired of Evan talking about the boy all the time. Harry grabbed his notebook and flipped through it. Page after page was unintelligible scribble. His own shorthand was something even he struggled to decipher on occasion. He stretched his arms out to pull his cuffs up and ease his shoulders a little. He started scribbling on a fresh page, and his frown lines deepened.

Harry looked at his list and felt better. He reached for the phone and dialled S O Davies' number. Harry had a lot of respect for the larger-than-life character who had been employed as a miner at the age of twelve and had been the MP for Merthyr since 1934. They arranged to meet in a quiet, atmospheric Cardiff pub, the Vulcan, between six and seven in the evening.

Staring into their pints, the two men talked about the forthcoming Aberfan report. As always, Harry was amused by the MP's peculiar habit of talking about himself in the third person. S O told him of the rumour that Richard Marsh, the

Minister of Power, wanted Lord Robens to resign as Chairman of the National Coal Board, although S O believed that Robens was quite safe. Due to the reorganisation in the coal industry, he was indispensable. They reminisced about the moment the news of the tip removal was announced outside the Welsh Office. Those members of the Canton Male Voice Choir on the staff at the Welsh Office had burst into 'Cwm Rhondda' in celebration of the good news. Harry had joined them in the singing, almost moved to tears at the second verse's 'Open thou the crystal fountain, Whence the healing streams shall flow'.

Harry spent another half an hour listening to S O rant about Harold Wilson. The Prime Minister's plan to remove the tips using money from the Disaster Fund was a disgrace and S O declared he was prepared to tell Wilson to his face. Harry didn't doubt him for a second.

"At least the rumour is that the report isn't a whitewash," S O said. "That's what S O was particularly afraid of. But, let's be honest, the mining industry was completely obsessed with its statutory duty to ensure as much underground safety as possible. It never thought about any potential hazard above ground. Left hand, right hand, eh? And all those previous tip slides. The possibility of it happening was clear. It absolves the community of any blame, which is good, because there has been too much finger-pointing. If you're asking S O, he believes that the Coal Board resented outside advice. But they won't get rid of Robens. They need him."

Before S O left, Harry asked him whether he knew of Doxsey.

"Know him?" S O asked. "He lost to S O in the general election in '64."

"He lost to you?"

"And he wasn't a graceful loser, either. Pretty sore about it, actually. He also lost to George Thomas in '66 when he went for Cardiff West."

"I know George. We're in the same choir."

"He lost badly to George. What's your interest in Doxsey?"

"I'm just checking him out."

"S O doesn't know much about his recent activities. You might want to speak to the Labour members of the council – David Evans and Iorwerth Jones. And not forgetting Lyons. They'll tell you about him. S O has the feeling they're not big fans of his. Ask them. There's nothing they don't know."

At two in the afternoon on the following day, the long-awaited copy of the Aberfan Tribunal report was delivered to Thomson House by courier, embargoed for twenty-four hours. Harry felt confident that the rest of the day would be productive, regardless of how long it might seem to drag. On the way to the pub to meet Julian, he composed the opening lines of his interview piece. He mentally swapped around the sentences as he walked. For a change, his anger toward the NCB eclipsed that which he projected at the Fleet Street press. Perhaps there wasn't any way for him to protect the people of Aberfan, but he could write something statesman-like, something the people of Wales would appreciate.

The report had found the Coal Board negligent as there had demonstrably been warnings of instability in the tips, but Harry was surprised that any potential sanctions were not in the scope of the report's remit. He had expected the tone to be more formal, legal even. He was surprised at how inclusive it was. He wondered whether the report itself – along with the moderate financial compensation – was to some extent meant to be a conciliatory gesture to the victims. That the villagers had been given a voice was deemed enough. Everyone who wanted to testify had been heard. Statements had been taken from 250 people. Harry felt that if the report was meant to be a token of reparation in itself, then it was deeply patronising to the Welsh. Acknowledgement the Coal Board was responsible was one thing, but heads should roll.

Harry and Julian had chosen to escape the newsroom for

the Horse and Groom. Above the bar were pictures of regulars holding up pints or smiling at the camera. Julian scanned the pictures, looking for Harry.

"I don't drink here often enough," Harry said, reading Julian's thoughts – though that didn't mean it wasn't one of Harry's favourites; he loved the fact that despite being across the road from Cardiff Castle, it had the feel of an old country pub.

Harry uncurled his copy of the report and gave it to Julian, having underlined the significant parts. Nothing had prepared Harry – not the shouts, digging, helicopters or claxons, nor the strange silence that had made him feel as though the horror rendered him temporarily deaf; nothing had prepared him for the fog lifting and seeing the thousands of volunteers. Finally, he had the report in his hands saying why.

Harry noted that tip seven had been sited in Easter 1958, without the NCB having any tipping policy with which to guide their choice of location. The NCB staffers chose a slope: a reckless decision on its own, even without taking into account the streams and spring clearly visible on any geological map. The report confirmed that warning letters had been sent to the NCB over the years. Tailings from the chemical process were described like oozing quicksand. Harry read on about communication problems and liquefaction: a coal tip can liquefy, become fluid, flow free and then re-solidify.

Between them, Harry and Julian drew up a list of potential angles for the newsdesk, with Harry dictating as the topics came up. He had already been making copious notes about the layout of the report. Soon the two of them were back at the office. Julian resumed his temporary perch at the end of Harry's desk, and both of them tapped furiously at their typewriters as the rest of the newspaper office caught up on reading the document. Now and again, Julian's attention would drift and Harry would throw balled-up spiked copy at him until the typing duel started again. For the next few hours, Harry didn't answer his ringing phone. Occasionally, one or the pair of them would stop to light a cigarette, which then burned unsmoked in the shared ashtray and spiralled up to join the bluish fog above them. Meanwhile, the news streamed around them, churning out on tickertape in the wire room and buzzing through the switchboard.

Harry decided to use the biggest quote in the introduction of his piece. The subs were going to run a picture of the disaster on the front page, but Harry demanded that it should be buried on page four.

"You write the stories. You don't get to choose the pictures," Huw said, trying to intervene in the argument.

"If they want pictures, then the pictures should be appropriate to the story."

They took the argument to Evan, who agreed with Harry's suggestion: a picture of Lord Robens of the National Coal Board would be on one side of the front page, and a picture of Lord Justice Edmund Davies, Chairman of the Government's Tribunal of Inquiry into the Aberfan Disaster, would be on the other. As for Julian's story, that was to be accompanied by a picture of people waiting to get their hands on the report outside the Stationery Office on St Mary Street.

Julian was thankful he hadn't been given more to write. Harry's writing, however, dominated pages four, five and six. When the paper was laid out, there didn't seem to be a centimetre of white space left. Harry wondered whether there was the possibility of preventing further publicity from finding Aberfan. That village has suffered enough, he thought, and prepared to head home. As Harry gathered his things together Julian commented on the legacy of the disaster. The old journalist did his best to be patient with the boy, who eventually got around to what was really bothering him: the fact that Harry hadn't invited him to meet S O.

"Look, son, I did you a favour," Harry said. "Last time I went to see S O, he was listening to the radio and these Welsh hymns came on. He insisted we both have a singalong and twenty minutes later we were still singing. It's lucky I knew the hymns from choir. You're English, or close enough. You don't know what you're getting into with S O. You don't need to hear his opinions on English journalists."

Harry liked to pause on opening his front door and guess or sense whether Bridget had visited. It made him feel as though he wasn't living alone. It was an act of reaching out for some signature or imprint in the silent house.

Bridget had unofficially gone to live with her sister years ago, but she continued to look after Harry. He never entertained the idea of finding someone else, perhaps due to their continued domesticity or the fact that his wife was far too staunchly Catholic to think of divorce. They told everyone that she had moved to keep her elder sister company and help with the kids. In reality, his work had taken over and she had become lonely.

While Harry's faith waned after Aberfan, hers would never falter. He realised how little they now had in common. His wife was becoming a stranger to him. Harry had no idea how to reach out to her, and living apart brought a sad calmness to both their lives. He couldn't imagine her back in the house permanently, but with her visiting two or three times a week, it wasn't as though he didn't see her at all. She hadn't completely abandoned him. Harry didn't know how Bridget felt about the situation. If he knew she was hurt over it, then he might have felt guilty, but for all he knew, she was happy with the status quo.

This time, there was a physical clue as to her presence. He bent to retrieve a grey sock at the foot of the stairs. Bridget had taken his laundry.

He went into the kitchen knowing she'd have left food under the tea towel. He lifted it off and draped it over the back of the kitchen chair and then put the oven on. He rested his hand on the piecrust, palm up, to feel for any warmth left in the food. There was none. He imagined Bridget's deft preparation, though he placed her in his kitchen rather than her sister's where she had undoubtedly put the meal together. The kitchen was where he missed his wife the most. She was a great cook and he missed the warmth of the oven, the act of arriving home and guessing from the scent of her baking what would be on offer. He missed her stews, her egg custards and her rice puddings. He still had them, though in a haphazard reheated fashion. Was it a punishment? Was she punishing them both? It was all such a mess. He didn't have much time and, impatient, he ate the food after it was half warmed by the oven. The kettle whistled brightly. Looking at the clock, he'd run out of time. He would have to grab a cup of tea when he got there.

Harry washed his face, changed his shirt and pulled on his claret blazer. He smoothed the front of his trousers down and ran a comb through his hair. His office might not be tidy, but he did his best to represent the *Echo* and the choir with his dress. He had his hair cut once a month and did his own ironing, just as he'd done even when he and Bridget were together.

He had been singing in the Canton Male Voice Choir for five years, watching the numbers steadily shrink until he had the idea of advertising in the Postbag. That was the only time he had used the Postbag for personal reasons. And it wasn't as though he had advertised for people. He had simply drafted a couple of paragraphs saying the choir would be proud to sing for the city and reminded readers that the group had been granted permission to wear the Coat of Arms. As a result of his writing, nine new members joined the choir and the bookings went up. It wasn't lost on Harry that the Arms depicted the commercial relationship between the Welsh mountains and the sea. What a dreadful mess that relationship was in at the moment.

It wasn't just the singing Harry enjoyed about the choir; it made a change from networking in pubs. Many boys from the Welsh Office had been attending longer than he had. He had lost count of the number of stories he'd gleaned from conversations in the twenty-minute tea breaks. Further, Harry loved the music. It was a challenge when they learned a new piece, but soon enough they would all be breathing together and the room would reverberate with sonorous harmony. There was something spiritual about it. As for faith, he certainly hadn't been back to church since that October in Aberfan. How long he'd attended like clockwork before the disaster, he couldn't say. Each day he walked past the church to his house opposite and glanced up at the dusty, sea-green circles of stained glass in the front tower. He was not tempted in the least to return. God's name was mud – Aberfan mud. Wasn't it Wilson who said he still hadn't cleaned the shoes he'd worn to Aberfan?

Harry arrived at their practice room earlier than he'd anticipated and chatted to a few of the other members.

Someone had left a copy of the *Echo* on the wooden chair next to him. He picked it up. The paper had been folded in such a way that the Ludlow-cast letters of 'ABERFAN' were impossible to miss. Harry was caught off guard; he felt as though he had written the story days ago. With the realisation that he was still involved in the same endless day, he felt a sudden exhaustion wash over him. It was then that Idris Evans came in and weaved around the room until he spotted Harry. Idris was a senior civil servant in the Information Division of the Welsh Office. Like Harry, his job involved newspapers, but in Idris' case, he combed daily through every newspaper, highlighting relevant stories to be clipped and filed or acted upon.

It was hard to tell how old Idris was with his smooth, pink, almost waxy skin and cheery blue eyes. It was only when he removed his hat and hung it on the coatrack that the shock of coarse white hair above his high forehead showed. Idris nodded and said a cheery hello as he tapped the newspaper.

"Just the man we're looking for," Idris said. "I was hoping you'd be in tonight."

"Problems at the Welsh Office?"

"Yes."

"Oh?"

"A problem with you. Come by my office in the week; we'll talk more."

Chapter 11

Harry, unable to concentrate, blew out a troubled cloud of cigarette smoke and slumped back in his chair. With the anniversary of Aberfan around the corner and the report out, he guessed it was something to do with the disaster. He resolved to mull everything over with a pint in the Press Bar, but he had a story to write first. After a marathon debate, the Abortion Bill had gone through by a majority of two to one. The Commons had cheered.

He looked at his clippings, coming up to a year old, yellowing in the carcinogenic haze of the newsroom. Some said Robens was a key part of the anti-nationalisation campaign: a yes-man to dismantle the mining industry. Dr Beeching was sacked for dismantling the railways, but Robens survived. Abnormal rainfall at Aberfan, they said. Trenches, ambulances, the grey stretchers, gas leaks, burst water mains. A race against time. Ghosts and lies. Doubletalk. Smokescreens.

Harry was interrupted from his reflections by an awareness that he was being watched.

"For God's sake, stop staring at me!" Harry said to Julian. "What do you want me to do?"

"Let's get out of here."

The pair left the office and walked down Westgate Street, Julian guessing correctly that they were heading for another pub. The Old Arcade's backrooms were being renovated, so they turned back onto St Mary Street. Harry led Julian to the upstairs lounge in the Blue Bell Inn. Harry was intrigued by the collection of Chinese landscape prints and resolved to ask the landlord about them. There were greyscale forests, snow-capped mountains, and waterfalls in mist and rain. Most colourful were the prints in which pagodas had been cast in the red glow of the rising sun. The dawn of communism, Harry supposed.

"If you're wondering why we're here," Harry said, "it's because I don't want anyone in the newsroom getting wind of this. I want to turn Doxsey over and you want to work in Fleet Street. Let's get you used to some old-fashioned Fleet Street investigative journalism. We'll need as much personal and business information as we can find."

"Where do we start?"

"We start with the most unpleasant of jobs, but it has to be done. Do you know where the best scoops often come from?" Harry said. "They come from a reporter who finds documents thrown out and discarded. News is what other people don't want you to find out."

"Thrown out and discarded? You want us to go through Doxsey's rubbish?"

"No, I want you to go through Doxsey's rubbish."

"How long for?"

"Once a week until you find something."

"What if I don't find anything?"

Harry made a resigned gesture with both hands.

"We'll play it by ear."

"Can't somebody else do it?"

"You need to get your hands dirty. You have to do a little fishing."

"This is a fishing trip?"

"That's exactly what it is. And we're after hooking a ten-pound Doxsey."

Julian paused.

"I'll need some rubber gloves," he said eventually.

Before leaving, Harry questioned the landlord about the artwork in the first-floor lounge. The prints were a gift from a generous Chinese friend. The landlord agreed that the red skies were indeed symbolic of communism. Rain, he informed

Harry, was associated in China with sadness, exile and disappointment.

Chapter 12

Harry parked up. The noises he made while locking his car and the sound of his feet hitting the pavement carried on the October breeze. The sky was turquoise with neon pink bands of cloud in the east, but the west was still a deep indigo. The lights of Thomson House were on, as they always were, and he smiled to himself.

Harry arrived to find George working himself up. It was unfortunate that a pedestrian article about budgies, written by Julian, had caught the ire of George. A trace of dried toothpaste in the left corner of his mouth suggested he had been in a rage before he'd left the house and was probably just looking for a convenient scapegoat.

After listening to a bout of incomprehensible swearing in which only a few regular words could be made out, words such as 'moulting' and 'old ladies', Harry decided not to engage in an argument defending his charge, who had yet to arrive. In truth, he felt a little responsible. Julian had no interest in budgies, but following his chat with Harry about content, had been keen to do a good job on whatever subject they threw at him.

The old journalist was surprised by how readily the Oxford graduate had taken up the bin proposal, and he felt touched by this blind obedience. The day before, Julian had obtained the rubbish collection times for Llandaff. The council collected the rubbish on Wednesday morning, which meant Julian was to rifle the contents of Doxsey's bin covertly on Tuesday night, every Tuesday night until he found something. Today was Thursday. Julian therefore had a number of days to plan the operation. Harry decided to divert the boy before he arrived into George's waiting ambush. When he saw Julian's car in the street, he headed down the stairs.

Harry greeted him in the foyer.

"What's up?" Julian asked.

"Nothing. Let's get breakfast in the staff canteen."

"You've seen the pool table, I suppose," Harry said, standing aside to allow Julian into the cafeteria first. "We have tournaments when Evan and Steve aren't around. Just don't let them catch you."

Harry loaded a tray with a weak mug of coffee for himself and an over-brewed tea for Julian. He popped three slices of toast, an envelope of butter and a small packet of strawberry jam on a plate.

"You're bright," Harry said, sitting down. "Journalism, it's a tool for positive social justice. That's my journalism, at any rate, but we're few and far between. I'm proud of what we do here. I want you to get a feel for that before you're gobbled up by the Fleet Street mentality, where they'll be issuing you with a company chequebook to buy stories and firing you if you don't get them. Maybe I'll never pin anything on these corrupt councillors, but if I knew that someone at the *Echo* was continuing to keep a wary eye out for these things..."

"Look, I can't do it."

"Keep an eye out?"

"This bin thing."

"I see," Harry said.

"Perhaps you can ask somebody else?"

"We'll talk about it later. Don't worry about it. All I'm saying is that you can make your name by establishing yourself on the local level before scrabbling up that ladder."

It was just as Julian was taking his first sip of brick-coloured tea that George walked in, glasses perched on the top of his head. He picked up a cup of coffee and a jam doughnut from the counter and then joined them at their table, stuffing half the doughnut into his mouth before he even sat down. Sugar and jam stuck to his lips and chin. He felt for his glasses, sat them in place and looked at Julian.

"Ah, our newest reporter," George said, licking around his mouth in wide swipes that also got rid of the toothpaste. "What the fuck was that budgie shit about?"

Julian stared at him. There were grains of sugar on the frame of his spectacles.

"Newsdesk asked for it."

"Budgies get lonely? Are you kidding me?"

"Now leave him be, George," Harry said.

While George licked his fingers as well as his mouth, Julian traced around one of the black squares in the chequerboard floor with his pointed boot and chewed his lip, nauseated. George popped the last bite of doughnut in his mouth and returned the stares of the seagulls watching them from outside the window. After wiping his fingers on his trousers, he raised his hands as though holding a gun and squinted through an imaginary sight. He took aim for a minute before turning back to Julian, still pointing his imaginary gun.

Julian also looked at the seagulls. Five fat birds were staring intently through the glass.

"Can they see us?" he asked.

"Don't change the fucking subject, or is that what your readers can look forward to next? This week: budgies. Next week: seagulls. Thrilling!"

Julian tapped his carton of cigarettes, took one out and lit it – drawing heavily. George snatched the packet from him and helped himself to one. Harry considered that George was never happier than when he was scaring someone. Nothing lifted the man's spirits like a combination of bullying, caffeine, nicotine and sugar.

After George had left, Harry looked at Julian.

"Don't take it personally. He's always been a prick."

Julian smoked his cigarette, resigned to the fact he was going to end up going through Doxsey's bins. Reading his face,

Harry assured him that he would know what to pick out from the councillor's refuse when he saw it.

After Julian left to interview an old lady whose house was being condemned, Harry finished making a permanent space for him at the end of his desk. Afterwards, he pulled out his box of awards and took stock. Among the collection was a dusty tankard. Harry picked it up, pulled a handkerchief square from his suit jacket and began to buff the tankard to a shine. It had been a present for his sixtieth birthday, the month before Aberfan. He hadn't wanted a fuss. Bridget had knitted him a new tank top and bought him some socks and slippers. She'd also baked him a cake and her sister had iced it. It would have been enough to stop there.

Whenever Harry's retirement came, it would not be voluntary. He knew Evan wondered about it. Although Harry told himself he was invaluable, common sense couldn't be avoided. On his sixtieth birthday, Evan had called him into his office.

"Right, old man. Whatever you do, be back here by five o'clock, right? Imagine, if you will, that our happiness depends on it."

"For...?"

"Five o'clock."

"No. What for?"

"Can't say, old man."

"I hope you haven't..."

"Got you a bottle of Grant's Whisky? Yes, old chap. You guessed correctly." Evan placed the drink – its neck prettily wrapped with a thick navy ribbon – on his desk. He pushed it towards Harry. "If you're not back in time, I'll fire you!"

"I can't promise—"

"Then I'll put your name forward for early retirement."

His birthday was synonymous with impending retirement. Editorial? They were predatorial. How many times would he be made to raise his glass and say 'Cheers!' to someone who wanted to jump into his position?

The party had commenced in the boardroom. He had been out interviewing someone and arrived back to find the secretaries had put up a banner and a tea trolley had been commandeered for Old Fashioneds, brandy and bottles of Brains.

When the ballad 'When a Man Loves a Woman' had come on the radio, a few of the reporters and subs had grabbed the female journalists, tele-ad girls, telephonists and secretaries and started to dance. Harry was grabbed himself by a female reporter called Sue. His dancing had been formal and a little self-conscious. They had fun, save for when one of the tele-ad girls found someone had inadvertently burned a cigarette-sized hole in her new pink dress. She had turned an angry red, welled up and walked out.

The party had later moved to the long, narrow bar of the Cardiff Cottage. Just as he'd begun to feel truly melancholy, the choir had trooped in. At least three quarters of them. He had been touched by that. And how they sang for him – until the barmaids finally remembered their other patrons and called for the singing to stop. Harry couldn't help but smile at the choir. He was at the beginning of his journey with them, rather than the end. He loved the camaraderie and found comfort in the polite way they addressed each other. There was something of the fairly recent war about their protocol: the regimental lines, politeness and blazers. There was a natural pecking order. The choir was essentially an extension of the Welsh Office. They'd all, including Harry, sung for Wilson when he visited Sophia Gardens Pavilion, and the Prime Minister had been touched by their impassioned rendition of 'We'll Keep a Welcome in the Hillside'. Harry, like the Welsh Office boys, shared an awareness of politics and scandal that rivalled most. He got many of their in-jokes. He watched the way the politicians positioned themselves. George Thomas, Minister of State, was tipped to take charge of the choir at some point. George was marginally more popular with the choir than at the Welsh Office, which wasn't saying much. George was like a hammy actor doing an impression of a Welsh politician, fawning over 'Mam' and insisting to the House that the faux pas of his wearing an Eton tie had been an innocent mistake and the offending article had been bought locally from the Co-operative store. Harry had long believed George Thomas peddled Welsh clichés, but the choir appreciated his knowledge of Welsh airs and hymns. His teaching career, after all, had started with singing at Marlborough Road Elementary School for Boys. Harry agreed with Jim Griffiths, the first Secretary of State for Wales, who said the Welsh had a hymn for every mood.

Throughout the evening of celebration, Harry had watched his colleagues taking note of the calibre of his friends in the choir. He wasn't over the hill yet. Even if he did retire, he would still be able to write. He could produce a newsletter of the choir's achievements, for example. In this way, he had told himself, he could retain something of his old occupation, still tell people 'I'm a former journalist with the *Echo*'. But he was getting ahead of himself, he reasoned. If he allied himself to the Welsh Office and the Welsh Office boys talked only to him, he could delay retirement. And any replacement would have to go to the ends of the earth to gather even half his contacts. It didn't even bother him – the fact that he suddenly needed the Welsh Office and their contacts when he'd never needed them before. That was life.

He had surveyed the pub full of journalists, his competitors and associates, those who would shake his hand, throw him a look of suspicion and ask him to treat this or that matter with delicacy. Everyone in their business had an agenda. All too soon, if he wasn't careful, he'd be old news.

Before being dropped home from work, Harry accompanied Julian on a reconnaissance mission: a drive past Doxsey's house on St Michael's Road. Julian would return alone after dark. The sun was just beginning to set – an autumn sunset – a sky of blue and gold. Julian eased off the accelerator and cruised past Doxsey's house before parking up. A black gate was wedged open by an ornamental stone. The drive was wide. There was a fresh coat of masonry magnolia and the windows sparkled. A clipped privet ran down to the front stone wall, separating Doxsey from his neighbour. A small bed of pink roses and miniature fir trees broke up the paved garden. Though some refuse was already out in the street, Doxsey's black bags had yet to join it.

"I'll be seen. That front wall is too low," Julian said.

"You'll have to grab the bags. Go through them somewhere else. Llandaff Fields, maybe."

Julian started the car in order to take Harry home and asked whether he would help him later.

"Not a chance."

Harry knew that the boy was annoyed with him. They didn't speak until they were at the lights on City Road.

"I wanted to ask you something," Julian said.

"Yes?" There was a pause. "Spit it out."

"What happened at Aberfan?"

Harry grunted as Julian turned the car onto his street. They came to a stop; he faced the young man at the wheel.

"It was a nightmare."

"George said—"

"Julian, never, ever start a conversation with 'George said'."

"You came back with nothing?"

Harry rooted around in his pockets for his house keys, found them and squeezed them in his hand.

"I was taught a lesson."

"What happened?"

"Friday, the day of the disaster, was terrible. The spill was difficult to navigate. I was wet through. It's not an excuse, but I was ill. I spent the night in a cinema. They had to get me a doctor."

Julian gave Harry a concerned nod.

"The next day, on the Saturday, I knew I had to get something for Evan and for the paper. The scene hadn't changed much, but they'd cleared out a good section of the school. Hydraulic posts were used to carry the weight of the roof. Men were still at the slurry. The fire service were dragging off masonry and boulders and breaking them up. It started to rain heavily and everyone was hoping that would put pay to the sightseers."

"Did you get out of there yourself?"

"No, that's my point. I had to find a good story before I came back. When I asked around, someone said that Miss Ann Jennings, the head teacher of the junior school, was alive and well. A few had seen her. Her account would have been the mother of all stories."

"Yes. Of course."

"I went looking for her. I managed to find a friend of hers who was looking for her, too. She told me that Miss Jennings was the founder member of the Soroptimist club she belonged to. She was there to drop off a cheque from the club for the disaster."

"What on earth is a Soroptimist?"

"I asked that myself. It's a club for women to help other women to get ahead."

"Feminists?"

"Probably, but very philanthropic. Anyway, this friend of hers said that only two days before, Miss Jennings gave this speech that in the event of a mining disaster, money from their emergency fund should be immediately released. She didn't want the rigmarole of calling all the members together in a crisis. This friend of hers said that as soon as she heard about the spill, she had written out their cheque for twenty-five pounds. She'd then come to look for Miss Jennings to see if she could help."

"That's a coincidence – her speeding up the release of money for a future mining disaster."

"It is. We teamed up looking for the head teacher. We found someone else who'd seen her but didn't know where she'd gone. Then we heard another story. Miss Jennings had received a petition at the start of the school year from two mothers. They complained about the black mud and water the children had to walk through on their way to school. Thirty-six parents had signed it."

"Right."

"She couldn't have known that months later the authors of that petition would have to identify their own children in the chapel."

"Oh no."

"We weren't the only people to hear this story. By that time, Fleet Street were all over it. They wanted to find out why she hadn't done more with the petition. They wanted to know what it was like being a head teacher witnessing that sort of devastation. Miss Jennings' friend left in the end because she was being harassed. I told her if I found Miss Jennings I'd let her know. The truth was, I was getting as desperate as Fleet Street."

"Did you find her?"

"Someone said she was on her way back to the school. There were so many people. You could hardly keep upright in that wet waste full of broken glass and matchboard shards. You also didn't want to look too hard at what you were walking in. It was chilling – a child's atlas or a broken doll – you didn't want to think."

"Miss Jennings was on her way to the school?"

"I waited along with half of Fleet Street. I told myself I would get the scoop. It was like the hunt was on and she was the prey. When none of us could find her, people started getting annoyed. We started to feel as though someone was messing us about. Two journalists got into a scuffle about it."

"You think she was keeping a low profile?"

"No, son. She wasn't hiding. An hour or two later, they gained access to her demolished room in the school. She'd been in there all along. She'd been doing paperwork in her room on Friday morning. Probably died instantly. It was all just rumour that she'd been seen alive. I couldn't carry on after that. I came back."

Harry gave a nod of his head to signal that was the end of the narrative. He got out of the car and saluted his goodbye. As he shut the car door, Julian leaned across the passenger seat and rolled down the window.

"Wait," he said. "Did Evan understand?"

"No," Harry said. "It's taken me until now to even talk about it."

Harry had not realised until Aberfan that humiliation came in many subtle forms. The idea that there might be people in Aberfan who had witnessed him impede the digging, fall ill in the cinema or try to secure an interview with a dead woman appalled him. And the idea of going back there again scared him. What if villagers remembered him? What if they confronted him about one of those incidents? He had so badly wanted to be an example of quality, caring journalism, yet the motivation behind his behaviour on the day of the disaster was so easily misinterpreted. What excuse could he ever offer?

When Julian entered the newsroom the next morning, Harry noticed him perk up at his new desk space. The boy threw down his bag, drew up his chair and nodded at Harry.

"How did it go?"

"I may have panicked a bit, Harry. It took me a while to calm down. I dragged the bags into Llandaff Fields, like you said. It was a revolting mess: mouldy apple cores, tealeaves and cigarette ends. I thankfully avoided getting covered in chip fat. Doxsey reads the *Echo*, you know."

"Of course he does. So you didn't get spotted?"

"The only interruption was a cat, but there was nothing in his rubbish. It was clean – in a manner of speaking."

"You look surprisingly happy for someone who's spent time rooting through bins."

"I enjoyed it in a funny way."

"I knew you were odd."

"I don't mean going through the rubbish. Maybe there's something liberating about being somewhere you shouldn't be. Seeing things from a different perspective. How many of my Oxford friends can say the same thing?"

"Odder still."

"No. I mean... I was thinking on the drive home – this is an interesting career. Of course it's going to mean doing dirty work from time to time."

Julian had performed the humiliating job too well and with too much spirit. It spoiled Harry's fun and negated the boy continuing.

"So you'll be disappointed that I won't need you to do it again?"

"Of course not. It was bloody disgusting."

At lunch, as they left the foyer of Thomson House for a bite to eat and a drink at the Press Bar, they heard the sound of shattering glass, a sharp smack and the clatter of something heavy hitting the pavement. Both journalists ducked and protected their faces with their hands. The two men turned to see what had happened, their hands still held aloft as though they were surrendering. On the pavement, a couple of feet away, there sat a battered Remington typewriter. Two keys had sprung loose and the impact had put a deep crease in one side. It was surrounded by shards of glass. Harry and Julian stood back on the pavement, looking up at a yawning gap in the first-floor windows.

"What the hell?" Harry shouted up. "You could have killed us, you fucking idiots!"

"What room is it?" Julian asked.

"I think it's sports. *Western Mail*."

The pair bolted up the stairs where a copytaker explained that the chief sportswriter had cracked up.

"He's stressed?" Harry said to Julian. "I may have had a wobble at Aberfan, but I never threw anything out a bloody window."

Chapter 13

Idris was sitting behind his desk at the Welsh Office, cross-legged with a letter balanced on his thigh. His head was inclined towards the correspondence and he had his elbow on his desk with the heel of his hand under his cheek. While Harry wasn't exactly sure about the particulars of Idris' job, he knew from conversations at choir that the civil servant addressed controversial correspondence. The contents of the letter on his lap, therefore, was of great interest to Harry.

Idris was so still that Harry wondered whether the old man had fallen asleep. Certainly, he sounded asleep. His breathing was deep and slow. Harry looked at the black and white prints of a Welsh seafront on the wall and wondered whether he should wake the old boy up. He could sympathise; despite Labour holding most of the Welsh constituencies, the Welsh Office had sizeable problems. The economy was floundering and the Welsh Language Society was keeping them pretty busy. The plan that Cledwyn Hughes, the Secretary of State, had come up with for devolution had needed to be reined in after Plaid Cymru had taken Carmarthen outright and sliced Labour's majority by over fourteen thousand votes in the Rhondda West by-election. They were still making progress, but nothing came easily. Then the Aberfan disaster happened. Harry imagined civil servants like Idris must have a permanent headache.

Idris raised his head and Harry realised that he hadn't been asleep – just thinking. Idris slid the letter across and rose to his feet. He walked to the wall and turned, stretching as he did so. Clasping his hands together, he watched Harry. The letter was dated 18 August and was written by Selwyn Jones, the Town Clerk of Merthyr Tydfil. It was addressed to the Secretary of

State for Wales. A line, underlined, read: 'Publicity at Aberfan'. The letter referred to a meeting of the council's General Purposes Committee where the continual coverage by television and press had been noted. The anniversary of the disaster, in two months' time, was expected to put the village back in the glare of media attention. The council appealed to the Secretary of State for any and all assistance to restrict press intrusion. Ah, Harry thought, Idris' comment at the choir wasn't about a problem with me at all. He was referring to a general press problem.

"What do you think?" Idris said, returning to his desk and offering Harry a cigarette before lighting one himself.

Harry cleared his throat and searched his pockets for his lighter.

"What's going on exactly?"

"This is all off the record. S O Davies has gone straight to Cledwyn Hughes. But, whatever you do, don't let S O know that I've told you about this. There's a freelance journalist poking his nose around Aberfan and this guy is getting too personal."

"In what way?"

"Prying into people's private lives. You can imagine the toll losing a child takes on a marriage. Well, this journalist, according to S O's source, is hoping a parent or two seeks solace in the arms of someone else from the village."

"For God's sake."

"He's also offering money to the first bereaved couple who conceive again, as long as he has the exclusive story and a photographer there at the delivery. The freelancer has already come to blows with another journalist who thought he was going too far. Come the anniversary, Aberfan will be crawling with these bastards."

"What are you going to do?"

"Oh, there are suggestions coming in from everywhere. Paul Marshall – I've worked with him for years in the Information Division but I don't think your paths have crossed – he had the idea of a rota party."

"A rota party. For the memorial service? Yes, I see. Cherry-pick journalists to report out to all the papers?"

"Including you, naturally."

Harry smiled politely but was too intrigued to be flattered.

"But we wouldn't choose them ourselves, you understand – save for throwing your name into the hat. Your feelings on Aberfan haven't gone unnoticed, you see. The rest would be left to the Newspaper Proprietors' Association and the Newspaper Society. And anyone stepping out of line will be immediately referred to the Press Council. The common suggestion is to get a team of journalists together. Six was the number quoted, I think. Six or seven – with the aim of having a frank discussion of this whole problem, perhaps calling in the Parents' Association as well, but you have to keep this quiet. This is off the record. Sidberry is drafting a letter to the Press Secretary for Number 10."

"Trevor Lloyd-Hughes?"

"Yes. Sidberry's already spoken to him. Very helpful. And Evan is adamant that we speak to Downing Street first before talking to everyone else. He's jumpy as hell."

"This is serious."

"Yes. That's what I wanted to talk to you about. You used to work in Fleet Street, didn't you? Put the feelers out. What are the chances of getting the press to lay off?"

"In Fleet Street?" Harry asked.

"Pay your old friends an unofficial visit. Be our ambassador for peace...?"

Harry absorbed what Idris was asking of him.

"I don't know. We're talking years—"

"You can get the ball rolling."

Idris, smiling, lifted both hands – palms up – towards Harry. He noted the gesture but didn't respond other than to lean forward.

"Are Downing Street really going to get involved?"

"Those I've spoken to are confident. Wilson's always had a bit of a hand in the press. We'll see how it goes. We're not asking for censorship. We're asking for a bit of sensitivity. This goes beyond Aberfan, of course. The image of Wales is being smashed to hell. The Welsh Tourist Board are precariously financed. Sludge and death, the Taff running black. That was one of yours, wasn't it? And you're supposedly on our side—"

"Yes, but—"

"That report shows the NCB was responsible, but the damage to Wales is a lasting legacy. The poison pen letters? And that piece you wrote about Edwards."

"Charles Edwards?"

"It was published on the sixth of August, I think. Did you check out the background to the story?"

"The father from Aberfan? It checked out. He lost a son in the disaster. He's ill with the stress of it. He's got ulcers."

"Well, I'm picking up information that there may be more to that. And it's not going to be a one-sided relationship between the Welsh Office and yourself. There has to be give and take in these things. A month after the disaster, we commissioned the Civil Defence to put together a report on the lessons to be learned after Aberfan. General Anderson's writing it – a very experienced officer. It will benefit a number of authorities, hopefully. It would be good if he has suggestions on controlling the national press following an incident. You'll be among the first to see it."

"I would be really interested in taking a look," Harry said.

"As I said, we want Wales' image back. Green valleys. The land of song. We can't have the Nationals pulling us apart again with their sob news. That village is in danger of being used for a decade, and Wales with it."

Harry could see Idris' concern was genuine. As he made to leave, the civil servant grabbed his arm at the door.

"You do understand, don't you? Westminster has ridden roughshod over us for years. I'm doing my best, in the most diplomatic terms, and I'm getting little for it. And then you've got Scotland forging ahead and being granted concessions at every turn."

Harry nodded, but Idris continued to squeeze the journalist's arm.

"Goronwy Daniel, the Permanent Secretary himself, has endorsed this – and this is all off the record, of course. Before Aberfan, we were fortunate. The London press barely noticed our existence. Goronwy is largely unheard of and hoping it stays that way. Cledwyn has less press than any other minister in Whitehall. Only the *Financial Times* has a Welsh correspondent and that suits us all just fine – for the moment."

"I know, Idris," Harry assured him.

The old journalist was aware that the mandarins in Whitehall were just waiting for the Welsh Office to make some irrevocable mistake. The moment they looked inadequate the whole thing would be pulled apart. You couldn't go a few months without departments splitting or new divisions being created. It was all so new and so fragile. And while it was, the Welsh Office wanted to remain under the radar.

Harry was thoughtful as he walked back to the *Echo* offices. The leaves were starting to fall and the Civic Centre was charmingly busy with students who exuded a confidence he hadn't had at that age. Harry had no idea what Idris had been getting at when he'd mentioned Charles Edwards. Perhaps there was more to the Disaster Fund story than Edwards had given him.

Harry was sceptical about the Government getting involved. What about freedom of the press? But the idea of a rota party, they could swing that, perhaps. It was routine for royal occasions, so why not the memorial service? Time was a problem, however. A collaborative newspaper campaign wasn't something he'd heard of before and it certainly couldn't be organised overnight. Even if it were possible, it would take many meetings and a great deal of persuasion. Aberfan was so terribly overused. He couldn't understand why the subs didn't speak up about such tacky sensationalism. Somebody certainly had to stop freelancers sniffing around for a scandal.

Harry was waiting for the lights to change in front of Cardiff Castle when he saw Labour's Dave Evans, councillor for the ward of Splott, hurrying towards him. Mr Evans might have had a tipple, judging by the pink flashes on his high cheekbones. He was clearly in a rush but raised his hat and smiled, happy to see Harry. They timed the traffic and hurried across.

"I need to have a chat with you and Iorwerth, your colleague," Harry said.

"And Iorwerth and I have got a few things you'll be interested in."

"I'll give you a ring. I'm after Sidney Doxsey."

"El Cid? That's what I wanted to have a chat with you about. I'd have thought the *Echo* would have been crawling all over him by now."

"How do you mean?"

"I wondered why the *Echo* hadn't picked it up. Phone me. Iorrie and I will fill you in." Evans looked at his watch, wondering if he could make a bit of time now, but shook his head. "We'll catch up soon."

Harry looked after him. He knew he couldn't let Doxsey escape, but he had bigger things to deal with now. He wondered how he would manage it all.

When Harry got back to the office both Evan and Julian were waiting for him. Harry smiled at them. Something told him that he should prepare first, but he was impatient and optimistic and his excitement was growing.

"The Aberfan memorial service, Evan," Harry said. "I suppose you'll want to cover it?"

"Of course we're bloody covering it." The editor gave a sharp laugh and presented a challenging grin. "Let's hear it."

"A thought occurred to me," Harry continued, unabashed.

"Do you think they've had too much publicity?"

"What are you saying, man? You've been obsessed about Aberfan and the NCB. Or are you saying that they've had more publicity than they deserve?"

"Bloody hell. Of course not. It's the bad publicity. Do you think they've possibly had too much bad publicity?"

Evan wrinkled his nose.

"It's really hard to get good publicity out of the death of innocent children, Harry."

"That's not what I'm saying."

Harry rubbed his index finger across his mouth, not sure if he should say more. He knew he should have trusted his instincts, but it was too late for that now.

"So what the hell are you saying?" Evan demanded.

"I think we should give them some peace. Not go too mad on the coverage."

"Oh, do you? I note you weren't complaining when we gave you three out of the five pages for the Aberfan report."

"That was hard news. The whole country wanted to know what was in the report. You saw them queuing down St Mary Street and the Gas Board in Merthyr was inundated. But the memorial service – that's not news. I'm thinking it's time to lay off."

"Of course it's news. And we'll be covering it. We'll be doing the 'One Year After' special, the same as everyone else."

"I know what's eating him," said George from his *Western Mail* desk, standing up and making his way over. "He's got subject fatigue. That's fine, Harry. Put the fucking information back in the library and let someone else have a go!"

"Okay, thanks George," Evan said.

"Yeah, thanks George," Harry repeated.

"But he's got a bloody point, Harry," Evan said. "Don't you want to write about Aberfan any longer?"

"No, I'm just thinking of the village. They've been through enough. It'll be splashed across all the papers yet again."

"Come on, Harry; the people of Aberfan are having the memorial service to remember last year."

George sat down on Harry's desk and adopted a thoughtful sneer, then said: "It's one year on. Do you think they want the world to pretend nothing happened?"

"They've only just had the report blaming the NCB," Evan said, "and might I add that all that shit you've got pasted to the wall is news. And it's all to do with Aberfan. What's this all about, anyway?"

Harry frowned and rubbed his hands as though cold. "Forget it. Listen, I'm thinking of visiting Fleet Street. I might take the boy with me.

Chapter 14

Harry's years of drinking meant he never had to endure serious suffering the day after a formal council dinner, but on this occasion, as the sun rose higher, he had no choice except to close his eyes to the blinding daylight, which rolled across the carriage floor like an empty wine bottle.

"Why didn't you go back?" Julian asked for what seemed like the tenth time.

Harry squinted out the window and lost himself in the landscape. A dirty huddle of white and tan ponies around a farm gate moved into focus and zipped off. Acres of fields, divided by lines of crooked trees and hedgerows, sailed up before being sucked away in a blur. The sky, cloudless and achingly blue, made him feel depressed. Now and again the craziness of the visit struck him. Was he really going to London to see if they would lay off? While the whole thing seemed preposterous, Harry reminded himself that Aberfan was the first time a disaster of that kind had been beamed by television into people's homes. And the story was about little children, for goodness' sake. Surely the usual rules didn't apply? Anything was possible. And what an extraordinary coup it would be if he pulled it off.

Julian was still waiting for an answer.

Harry closed his eyes again, then replied: "I don't know why I left, not when the place I live now has banned *Ulysses*."

The pair didn't talk again until the scenery was transformed and they were racing past industry; weed-edged yards, dandelions and dock weeds; piles of old tires, rusting machinery; corrugated roofs, wire fences. Eventually they came to black brick terraces and high rises with washing hung to dry against the sunlit windows. The clothes and sheets looked faded and old in the bright light. Fifteen minutes later, they arrived at Paddington.

Ah! How delighted Harry was to see the old landmarks from Fleet Street: St Paul's and the spire of St Martin's. And what weather they were having. It was hot enough to encourage hopeful talk of an Indian summer. Julian took in the Royal Courts of Justice as Londoners fanned themselves. They were running a little late and Harry started to pant with the effort. They stuck to sticky shade on the south side of Fleet Street until they reached El Vino's black and gold frontage at the junction with Fetter Lane.

"It's lucky Bower's not here," Harry said to Julian, referring to El Vino's feisty owner as they entered the bar and restaurant. "He'd ban you on the spot."

The ceiling fans did little more than blow warm air around a dining room of various browns. The bright light cast from the pendants above bounced off the polished glass frames of old illustrations and sepia maps. Wine bottles and copper jugs littered a picture rail and a mantelpiece too crowded by furniture to be used. A blackboard of specials hung above the counter. The smell of red wine and roasting meat freely circulated. A man sitting at a table waved them over, fanning himself with the menu in his other hand.

"Are you okay, old boy?" Tom asked as the two *Echo* journalists manoeuvred their way around the tables and chairs.

"Never better. Good timing, eh?" Harry said, picking up Tom's empty wineglass.

Harry and Tom had lost contact a number of years ago. For a long time, Harry had wanted to meet his Fleet Street friend to get the inside on *The Chronicle* and *The Star*, but Tom had often been busy and it never seemed like the right time. This time, Harry had twisted his arm. The fact that the *Echo* was paying helped.

Julian couldn't have chosen which of the two men before him needed a drink more. Harry was sweating through his shirt.

As if reading Julian's mind, he pulled a handkerchief from his pocket, removed his hat and dabbed his forehead. Tom, on the other hand, looked ill, almost grey. In the midst of their introduction, Tom had a coughing fit. A sympathetic waitress arrived with a glass of water. After Tom breathlessly lapped it up and his wheezing dissipated, he blamed his ill health on overwork. Fleet Street, he assured Harry while lighting a cigarette, got more demanding, not less.

Tom took a pointed glance at his watch and then looked enquiringly at the Welsh journalists.

"It's been a long time, Harry. To what do I owe the pleasure?"

Harry noticed there was no effort to conceal the impatience in his former colleague's words. Was he already in a hurry to get rid of them?

The meal was over quickly and Harry persuaded Tom to join them for a drink, hoping he would get an opportunity to raise the subject of Aberfan. They headed for Ye Olde Cheshire Cheese on Wine Office Court. Tom gave Julian a potted history. Charles Dickens had been a regular visitor. Harry looked for any sign of change since his exile but saw only the same amber gas lamps and sawdust collected like snow in dark corners. The three journalists ducked down when they entered the vaulted cellar. The wall sconces ineffectually threw out small pools of yellow light into the gloom and it was gloriously cool. Most of the tables were taken, so they sat in a row on a church pew. Harry, in the middle, was the first to think of the three wise monkeys: a terrible mantra for journalists. He was 'see no evil'. Heaven forbid, he thought. What would be left to write about?

Harry felt good to see Tom, though he appeared quite distracted. The Welsh journalist tried to think of something to remind him of their friendship. Eventually, Harry asked what car he was driving. The answer was an Alfa Romeo Giulia, but Tom now had his sights on a black Audi Super 90. Julian sat forward enthusiastically, but then sank back as Tom launched into a seemingly endless rant about the parking in Fleet Street:

"Sixpence for half an hour. It's outrageous!" Tom said, and then cited a number of London journalists who had been caught out.

He's warming up, Harry thought, and so continued to remind Tom of their old connection by asking about their shared history. When Tom finally paused for breath, Harry asked how he'd fared at the *Mail* after *The Chronicle* folded – given the two papers' disagreement on Suez, among other things. Tom stubbed out his cigarette and frowned. Harry had clearly strayed into unwelcome territory, but rather than close the Fleet Street journalist down, it did the trick. Tom suddenly became very animated:

"Yes. The *Daily Mail* took me on. Lucky me. The only good thing to come out of it is that I managed to jump ship for the *Express*. Julian, I doubt Harry knows this pearl of wisdom, but everyone here knows that anyone who gets sacked from the *Mail* can get a job on the *Express* and anyone who gets sacked from the *Express* can get a job on the *Mail*, within reason."

"It's been that way as long as I can remember," Harry said.

"Maybe I'm exaggerating a little. They're not going to hire you at the *Mail* if you've strangled the editor of the *Express*, or at least not until the criminal case is over. Anyway, the problem was that the editor at the *Mail* hated me – politics, you know how it is. The guy on the newsdesk also had an extremely quirky view of things. He'd get all hot and bothered about stupid stories like lookalikes..."

"Lookalikes?" Julian said.

Nodding, Tom drank a third of a pint and wiped his mouth, all the while drawing circles in the air with his free hand to indicate that the conversation was about to progress.

"Yes, you know... someone in a pub being a lookalike for a famous darts player or Clint Eastwood. He'd come in the next morning and get one of us to follow things up. It was bloody frustrating. Told him I'd quit Fleet Street to work on my masterpiece. Do you know what the son of a bitch said? Never mind. No point dragging it all up again. Doctor says it's bad for my health."

"We're hearing all sorts of things," Harry said.

"You missed the NUJ in Southsea. It was all about automation. The coaxial cable will change the playing field. Electronic scanners. Mark my words, Julian, things are about to undergo a revolution in the media. Take the *Daily Mirror*. Those rotaries are churning out five million copies a day. Why not scan it to the provinces and let them do the bloody printing? They'll break the unions to do it. They'll have to."

"That's my dream job," Julian said. "The *Mirror*."

Tom grimaced and looked at Harry, who was growing concerned about how he was going to get rid of the boy in order to have a proper conversation with his Fleet Street contact.

"I'm sure Harry is a bigshot in Wales," he said to Julian.

"What does that mean?" Harry said.

"If Julian wants a job with the *Mirror*, then you need to talk to someone who works there," Tom said.

The three of them sat in silence for a moment.

Tom lifted and shook his empty packet of Pall Mall to indicate, rather too blatantly to Harry's mind, that he had run out of cigarettes. Harry fished out three shillings and eleven pence and handed the money over. Julian went to head for the vending machine but Harry called him back and pointed out that they were too expensive and the newsagent was cheaper. They watched Julian vanish up the stairs.

"Babysitting?" Tom asked.

"He's the nephew of the managing director."

"I can't get him a job, you know," Tom said. "Nothing going."

"I wasn't going to ask," Harry said, looking around the room quizzically. "I need to ask your advice."

"Oh?"

"Aberfan. This is all off the record. Do you think there's any chance of one of the Nationals picking up a campaign to get folks to lay off Aberfan? The *Mirror* would, surely?"

Tom narrowed his eyes, giving Harry a canny, suspicious look.

"For the anniversary?"

"Yes."

Tom sat back thoughtfully and took a sip of beer.

"Why the *Mirror* in particular?"

"I don't know. Maybe because we've been talking about it. Maybe because Hugh Cudlipp is Welsh. Who knows?"

"And you mean to keep the press away?"

"Yes. You know what it'll look like. TV crews standing on the site of the school, wringing out every ounce of emotion from the tragedy."

"Ah."

The pair sat in silence for a moment, thinking.

"Doesn't it make sense that one of the Nationals could inspire the others to respectfully give the villagers a break?"

Tom shook his head and laughed.

"It's worse than I thought. You lasted what? A couple of months in Fleet Street? You're honestly telling me that you want to coordinate a shutdown of the London press? You and whose army?"

"This has nothing to do with how long I worked here. It has very little to do with me at all. I'm just the messenger."

"Fleet Street chewed you up and spat you out. And here you are again like Don Quixote!"

Tom laughed until he started to cough and then lit another cigarette.

"I wouldn't put it like that," Harry said.

"You've tickled me, I'll give you that. Look, I don't know why I have to spell this out to you. Every editor is his own man. And who would you persuade? Even if you got a journalist or an editor or two to buy it, they'd have to contend with the rest of the people on the paper. And let's say, miracle of miracles, you persuade one paper to agree – then the rest wouldn't follow. They'd call you a bunch of idiots and probably run with the line that the lessons of Aberfan must not be forgotten. Here's a question, are you going to lay off Aberfan?"

"I would if I could."

"So you're not?"

"I tested the water, but it's not me they're worried about. It's London and the foreign press we need to worry about."

"Interesting. Who's the 'we'?"

Harry looked at him and bit his lower lip, thinking.

"Wales," he said.

"I'm sorry to say it, but you've lost touch. Half of Britain donated money to the Disaster Fund," Tom said. "The whole country was up in arms about it and the whole country will want to read about it when the memorial service goes ahead."

Tom was vehement but amused. Harry was acutely aware that Julian was due back any minute. If Tom continued to talk about this in front of Julian, it might get very awkward.

"You can't tell me you weren't appalled at the coverage by your own paper last Sunday. The parents of Aberfan, I quote, 'squabble and fight while their sons and daughters suffer', and not forgetting the astonishing line, 'the children of Aberfan are guilty of being alive in a village where one hundred and sixteen children died'. Tom, they are victimised because they are alive!" Harry leaned forward towards him, his eyes wide and fingers splayed: a quick gesture of shocked appeal.

"You know what it's like, Harry. Some journalist finds a different angle and the rest of Fleet Street charges down there to find out if it's true or not. It'll calm down."

"I'd be grateful if you don't mention this to little Lord Fauntleroy," Harry said, noting Julian coming down the stairs. He relaxed his posture.

"He's the nephew of the managing director, eh? Well, let's introduce him properly to Fleet Street journalism – as long as you're paying."

"And absolutely don't mention it to anyone you work with."

"They wouldn't believe me, anyway."

Julian dropped the packet of cigarettes in front of Tom. The veteran journalists continued their small talk but only for the boy's sake.

"I read in *The Times* that ITN have poached Wallington for Monday night news."

"Is that right?" Harry asked, more tersely than he intended.

"Let's take him to the Old Bell next."

"If you like," Harry said, getting up.

Julian, unsteady on his feet, surveyed the front of Ye Old Bell Tavern with a drunkenly sentimental smile, not that he had been there before. He raised his arms in a welcoming gesture at the grand old stained glass with its rubies, topaz and emeralds. A series of lamps in the shape of bells lit the glass from above. Harry took solace in the fun they were having with the young man. Inside, Julian badly negotiated the sloping floor which had buckled with age. The pair ordered more beer and sat Julian directly at the front window where they watched the London street distort and twinkle through the glass.

"He hated me in the beginning," slurred Julian.

"What? Harry? I don't believe it for a second," Tom said.

"Ignore him," Harry said. "He's drunk."

"He did. Because I went to Oxford. But now I'm helping him fight local corruption."

Harry shook his head with a smile.

"He doesn't appear to hate you now," Tom observed.

"That's because he has taken the time to get to know me."

Harry couldn't help but laugh.

"Will you stay at the *Echo* for a while, do you think?" Tom said.

"God no! I want to work in Fleet Street as soon as possible," Julian replied.

"So much for your fight against local white-collar crime. I wouldn't give up just yet. Corruption may be the next zeitgeist.

There are rumours in Fleet Street about an architect called Poulson. Corrupt to the core, so they say. He's allegedly had his hand in every council till you can think of. Potentially a major splash. You heard it here first. This is a proper induction to Fleet Street working practices."

The two veteran journalists drained their pints and simultaneously banged down their empty glasses.

"Wait. Wait," Julian said as they stood up. "It was hard, Harry, the way you gave me the cold shoulder." He stared hard into one of the empties, as if some scene of his future London career was being shown to him. "Would you put a word in for me, Tom? When the time's right?"

"I don't know yet."

With Julian too drunk to follow their conversation, Tom opened up with more detail about Cecil King – the Chairman of the *Mirror* – and his troubled relationship with the Prime Minister. Harry listened.

On the last train home, as Julian snored softly, Harry was thoughtful. God, he hadn't missed Fleet Street at all. Tired, with the glimmering of a headache in the background, he mused how the London journalists were full of themselves.

If the Welsh press couldn't manage it, then who could? Although, on the other hand, perhaps they could embarrass any national papers that exploited Aberfan. Actually embarrass them! Any journalists going too far would be featured negatively in the papers for the people of Wales to read about. He kicked himself again for raising the matter with Evan so quickly. His approach to his editor needed to be more considered. Still, there were two things he could get underway immediately, though he'd enjoy the first more than the second.

Julian opened his eyes a little.

"How are you doing, son?"

"I feel terrible."

"Well, sort yourself out, because when we get back you're

going to focus on Doxsey. You're going to eat, sleep and breathe that corrupt car salesman."

"Me? I thought I was following your lead?"

"I can't, son. Something has come up."

"What's going on, Harry?"

"I've got total faith in you." Harry paused. "But didn't you have something to tell me about Doxsey? Do you remember? I was a bit busy at the time."

"Did I?"

"Yes. The first day we worked together."

Julian had been lying on his side across the seats from Harry but dragged himself into a half-seated position.

"Oh, that? You weren't interested." Julian had quite forgotten until Harry reminded him. "It was when I was outside Doxsey's office. The receptionist said something about planning. Some council complaint and Mr Doxsey was refusing to take the call—"

Julian quickly excused himself and headed for the toilet, saying he felt ill. When he returned, Harry noted that he looked grey.

"Have you been sick?"

"Don't talk about it," Julian said, sitting down gingerly.

The boy flicked through his notebook. There it was: 'Mary Hallinan'. He handed the notebook to Harry and pressed his hand against the window in what Harry assumed was an attempt to still himself against the rocking of the train.

"I think you'd better..." Harry gave the boy a little shooing motion with the notebook he'd just been given.

Julian clamped a hand over his mouth and lurched off.

Chapter 15

The next morning, Harry, tired from the day before, pulled back the bedroom curtains to find the street cold and peaceful. The first of the autumn storms predicted for the week had come to nothing, but when he arrived at work, he noticed an ominous bank of black cloud was building to the south.

"You look terrible," Harry said as Julian approached their shared desk.

"Don't even ask. And to top it off, I've got to meet my girlfriend this evening for a talk."

"Someone's in trouble."

"We've only been going out three months. She's from Cardiff. A bit of a hippy. I met her in the Quebec. We're both fans of the Icon Jazzmen. Have you heard of them?"

"No."

"I'm a sucker for them."

"Icon Jazzmen?"

"Hippy types: patchouli, patchwork velvet, that sort of thing. She likes screen prints. Her hands are always stained with primary colours. But whatever they tell you about this peace and love philosophy, the hippy girls are the craziest. They can be pretty judgemental, too."

"Maybe it's not what you think."

"She's going to dump me soon, and when she does, I bet she won't be peaceful or loving."

"Wait until you've been married as long as I have."

"At least you're still together. What's so important that you can't work on Doxsey?" Julian pressed his temples with the palms of his hands. "I can't go on my own. I feel awful."

"I'll come and see Mary Hallinan with you and then I've got to get back. I've got to write a piece on bonsai. Evan's gone mad for them. He wants a 'Try a Tree Inside Your House' story. I've got to bone up on Japanese horticulture."

They were out of Thomson House in less than twenty minutes. The storm finally hit on the way to Mary Hallinan's house. Any glimmer of sun was quickly chased away with hurled leaves and litter. Windblown umbrellas were waved about furiously and then abandoned to the gutters. Branches were brought down. Everything was streaked and stained with rainwater save for the autumn leaves, lifting and swirling every so often in the racing wind like shoals of bright brown and orange fish.

The wall which ran down the side of Mary's front garden was black with rainwater, and studded here and there were tiny ferns growing out of the cracks. Harry, holding his hood in place, walked to the gate to see if the curtains were moving and was relieved when he saw the plump shape of Mary Hallinan moving behind the glass of the rain-sprayed front door.

They hung up their dripping coats and Mary led them through the house with a warning that it was in a bit of a mess. The kitchen was airy and fragrant with the smell of fresh tea and buttered toast. Julian's face paled at the same time his stomach growled and Harry quietly asked him if he was all right.

The breakfast table was invitingly full: cosied tea pot, china cups, marmalade, and an empty silver toast rack with golden crumbs beneath. *The Times* newspaper lay folded with the crossword completed in capital letters. Mary's husband, Lincoln, wearing a charcoal suit, came into the kitchen and exchanged pleasantries with Harry. He shook hands with Julian and explained that he'd been telling his wife she should have done this much sooner. Before leaving for work, he gave his wife a kiss on the check and knelt down to smooth the ears of an aged honey-coloured Spaniel, mumbling baby talk to it. The Spaniel whined sadly. Mary Hallinan poured tea as the rain rattling the windows made the scene even homelier.

"Come into the reception," Mary said, when her husband had gone.

The pair had been content in the kitchen but they carried their tea into the cold reception room where, already damp, Harry shivered. Mary Hallinan left them alone for a few minutes while she righted the kitchen. The only splash of colour came from a maidenhair fern, trembling in the draft from the bay window. Mary swept back in, wiping her hands on a check tea towel which she threw over the arm of the sofa.

"How did you know to speak to me?" Mary said, smoothing her short grey hair.

"I was in Doxsey's office when you called once," Julian explained.

"That must have been a while ago. I've been to the police since."

"You've talked to the police?" Harry said.

Mary's eyes widened and she wrinkled her nose.

"I didn't want to, but he left me no choice."

Harry turned to a fresh sheet in his notebook.

"What's it all about?"

"You mean to tell me you don't know?"

"We've had hints, but we're trying to put the pieces together."

"There's a shortage of sites for petrol stations. Petroleum companies are willing to pay high prices, especially when there's prior planning permission. Doxsey's been playing ducks and drakes in the Planning Committee – playing both sides on a proposed plan for Crwys Road and another site in his own ward."

Harry looked up from his notebook.

"Can he do that?" Julian said.

"Of course," Harry said, "if he's not averse to criminal tactics."

"He's got two options," Mary continued. "He could make his wishes clear on a specific development to a paid official or he could influence the council chamber. It's my belief that he tried both. I got suspicious. Especially when he came to visit me."

"Here?"

"Yes. Twice. The second time it was a Sunday evening, a week before the Planning Committee met."

"What was his visit about?"

"He said I was playing into Labour's hands if I got in the way."

"When did all this happen?"

"Last summer. The council confirmed the application had been refused in early April of last year. Then in early May, the game changed completely. May last year, do you remember what happened?"

Harry smiled and nodded. "The Conservative Party got a majority in the municipal elections."

"He's the Conservative Chief Whip. That same day, and only six weeks after the application was rejected, a fresh application was submitted."

"Well, I'll be," Julian said.

Having bumped into David Evans outside Cardiff Castle before his trip to London, Harry had since arranged a meeting for that afternoon in the Rummer Tavern on Duke Street. The plan had been to let Julian conduct the interview with Evans by himself. However, Harry changed his mind when the boy pressed him about why he was being left to handle the whole Doxsey story alone.

The upstairs lounge was Harry's first choice; it afforded a lovely view of Cardiff Castle, but a jolly group were already at his favourite table, and so the two *Echo* journalists and their contacts remained downstairs in the bar.

"Any woman that gives up university to campaign for Callaghan is fine by us!" Iorwerth said, raising his glass.

"Mr Morgan here," David Evans said, indicating a young

man with a mop of curly hair and a colourful taste in ties, "has just made an honest woman of Julie Edwards."

David Evans and Iorwerth Jones were an inseparable pair of Labour councillors. Similarly dressed in sombre suits and Buddy Holly glasses, they lived for party gossip and delighted in stirring up trouble for the other parties. The hot topic of the day was a councillor they alleged was having an affair with a young lady from an opposition party.

"Love transcends politics," said Harry.

"No," Iorrie returned, grinning. "Sex transcends politics!"

"Fair enough," Harry agreed, laughing.

"If you're wondering why we delayed this meeting, we were waiting for Rhodri here to get back from his honeymoon."

"Congratulations," Julian said.

Rhodri smiled, thanked Julian and introduced himself properly. Harry had heard of him. He was tipped for great things in the Labour Party and was another worthwhile contact.

They all skirted around various other bits of tittle-tattle. Eventually, Harry drew the conversation around to Doxsey.

"Doxsey's lost the plot," David Evans said, with a look of barely contained amusement. "We didn't use the Whip. We don't have to for petrol stations. Labour never votes for them if they're on corners. Doxsey's accusing us and Ted Rowlands of involving Scotland Yard, but it was Councillor Hallinan. Doxsey is determined that it's a Labour setup."

"Scotland Yard are involved?" Julian asked.

"They've only just been called in. I don't think they've even interviewed Doxsey yet. All that slum clearance. All the new builds. Somebody's making lots of money."

"So he's going to be charged?" Harry said, looking at Julian.

"Looks like it," Iorwerth said. "I had one hell of a row with him over the planning application. And you'll want to know why we've brought Rhodri along."

Rhodri Morgan put down his pint and smiled.

"Harry," Rhodri said, "you should be aware of something

else about Doxsey. Cledwyn sent out maps of the proposed boundary changes to all the Cardiff city councillors. There was a reshuffle to make voting fairer. You know how it is, I'm sure. So Sidney Doxsey receives his map and you know what he does?"

"What?"

"He redraws some of the boundaries!"

Harry watched as Rhodri sketched around imaginary ward boundaries on the pub table.

"You're joking," Harry said.

"Honestly. Not for his ward – that would be too obvious – but he redraws other boundaries in Cardiff to give the Tories a nice big voting advantage. The man was flat out having a go at gerrymandering! He alters the boundaries and sends it back. It was a colleague of mine who spotted it. We'd never seen anything like it. I had to report it to Callaghan."

"We'll have another chat with him," Harry said.

"Isn't this what you've been after for years?" Iorwerth said.

Harry smiled and nodded thoughtfully.

Harry, despite his preoccupations, briefed Julian on the next steps to be taken for the Doxsey story and encouraged him to pay another visit to the councillor alone. Later that afternoon, he was surprised to learn Doxsey had agreed to meet Julian within an hour. Harry wondered who Doxsey's legal representative was and it occurred to him that he might not have appointed one yet. So much the better, Harry thought.

Julian found that Iorwerth had been right; Doxsey insisted it was Labour who were corrupt, and he was adamant the local Labour group voted en bloc against big development.

"You wouldn't think it," Doxsey said, "but planning applications are often debated and discussed." Trying to hint at a potentially bigger story for the *South Wales Echo*, he went on to suggest that Detective Chief Inspector Mooney was Labour as well. "They're all in on it. That is the real story. And they are in the wrong," he told Julian, cocking his head to one side. "They got the Labour Chief Whip to encourage the Labour members of the Planning Committee to vote against Conservative members applying for planning. Was I supposed to just sit back and let it happen? But the bottom line is this: Iorwerth has a bee in his bonnet. I am that bee. I am the bee in Iorwerth's bonnet."

Julian suppressed a smile.

"It wasn't just about the money," Doxsey said. "It was about clearing up a rat-infested eyesore. If the Crwys Road site isn't developed, it'll become a health hazard. As a councillor, that was my main priority."

"But Mary Hallinan disagreed?"

"This is a democracy. She has the right to disagree. It's a free country. And I'm not going to say a word about nationalist narcissism or Labour using underhand tactics to shut down honest Tory business in Wales. She was blind."

"And what about the suggestion that you were telling people it would ruin you?"

"Now that's just not true. I think it's time we wrapped this up."

Doxsey stood and gestured politely towards the door.

"One more thing. Scotland Yard, have they spoken to you yet?"

"No. And don't you think it's strange that our learned police authority are uncomfortable dealing with this?"

Julian shrugged after standing up.

"It's funny," Julian said on his way out, "that if you hadn't have banned that film you wouldn't have attracted so much attention at the *Echo*."

"It wouldn't have stopped the Labour smear. Anyway, I was protecting people."

"Oh, and I was in the pub the other day and I heard you tried a spot of gerrymandering over ward boundaries."

"Are you kidding me? You're too young to appreciate what

this is about. And there I was thinking the youth of today were idealists. I'm developing sites and areas of land that would otherwise be a target for fly-tippers, graffiti artists and home to a growing number of rats and birds. I'm a man of vision. I'm thinking of the economy. The local environment. You think this ridiculous case will ever stand up in court? Think again!"

Julian shrugged and left.

Chapter 16

A group of young boys in front of Harry and Julian were pretending to be shot and they died theatrically to the sound of gunfire coming from inside the castle.

The storm had passed in time for the city to start preparing for the Cardiff Searchlight Tattoo and Harry and Julian were told to call in. The *Echo* had other reporters covering it, but Evan had decided the experience would be good for Julian, and they had been given an excess of press passes, anyway. Harry also hoped the festivities might perk the boy up, preoccupied as he was with his visit to London.

The old journalist's own ambitions for the Lay Off Aberfan campaign, mulled over on the train back, seemed to have been left at the station. His faith that the *Echo* would support him had vanished. Initially, the rebuff from Fleet Street had made him stubborn, angry and even more determined to take the situation in hand, but deep down he knew the task was probably futile. He mused on how determination waxed and waned and he hoped a little of his old confidence and fighting spirit would return. He worried that if he continued recklessly, the whole thing would come to nothing or end up with his career in flames.

Harry and Julian looked at the programme outside the castle as crowds funnelled through the arched gate. It felt to Harry more like spring. His face tingled in the peppermint-fresh air. The sky was a lattice of thin white clouds reminding him of cheerful blue gingham. The old ladies of Cardiff had seized their last chance to don their summer clothes, cold though it was, before the time came to pack away their pastel macs and pillbox hats of ruffled lace or organza. With the old ladies trailed wafts of lily-of-the-valley and Yardley English Lavender, and a good number were shepherding tottering grandchildren in hand-knitted bonnets. Harry kicked himself for not thinking to invite Bridget and his nephews. Bright lads. One day he'd try to get them into the news industry – if that's what they wanted.

First on the roster was community singing, accompanied by the band of the South Wales Borderers. A fanfare of trumpets was to follow it. Bands would perform a parade and then there would be an exhibition of motorcycle riding by the Royal Corps Military Police – by kind permission of the Provost Major. There was a pageant of past, present and future, and a display of close combat that was entitled 'You've Had It – Chum!' There was an array of military hardware: howitzers and a helicopter. A man on a penny-farthing raced in circles, red coattails jangling behind him, waving a hand at the crowd like a circus clown.

Most of Cardiff had turned out. Broad-shouldered men hoisted duffel-coated children onto their shoulders. Young women in daisy-print or polka-dot shifts walked arm in arm with lively lads – all checked shirts, Chelsea boots and scruffy hair – who stared moodily and muttered, as the displays began, that they could do a lot better than these fucking soldier boys.

Harry recognised Major Jackman, who'd been running the event for the last four years. Another Englishman running a Welsh event, Harry thought. He directed the journalists to the press hut: a trailer on stilts. Harry climbed the steps and swung the door ajar. George was deep in conversation with a military press officer. Harry couldn't remember his name but recognised him by his red beard. Another five journalists were pouring themselves drinks. The trailer was stuffy and already smelled like a pub ashtray. Bottles were everywhere – beer, wine, spirits and mixers. There was even a jar of sliced lemons.

Harry and Julian took a beer each and decided they would watch the parade for a couple of hours, stay for the motorcyclists and then head back to the office.

"What's this thing between you and George, then?" Julian asked.

"We fell out big time about three years ago."

"Over what?"

"A duck."

"Come again?"

"You know. A duck? Quack, quack? Yellow thing. Floats in the bath?"

Julian laughed. "You're making no sense."

"Remember that really hot summer we had three years ago? We had all the fans going. All the copy had to be weighed down to stop it blowing everywhere."

"Okay."

"I don't know where the duck came from. It used to live on a shelf gathering dust. George, being a juvenile prick, invented this ridiculous game. He'd throw the duck at a ceiling fan and the bird would shoot in whatever direction the fan batted it."

"I get it. It's a play on words, right? Everyone has to duck from the duck?"

"Yes. Exactly. But I was too busy to play. I had a deadline."

"So you got rid of the duck?"

"Something like that."

"That can't be the reason."

"Of course it can. As I said, he's an arrogant, juvenile prick."

"But it can't be the reason you still hate each other. Because you stole his duck? Come on. What's the real reason?"

"All right." Harry rolled his eyes and thought for a second. "I don't want you discussing this with anyone, but George has a wife and five daughters."

"I know."

"He's also a serial womaniser."

"Is he?"

"It's hard to believe, I know. Speaking of women, how did the talk go with your girlfriend?"

"She's my girlfriend no more. She called me bourgeois –

among other things."

"You're just a bit posh."

"I'm not *that* posh."

"The longer you work at the *Echo*, the less posh you'll be."

I'm having a delightful day, thought Harry, gazing happily around the pageantry. He only wished that his mind would stop remembering his enquiry to Tom and the way he'd laughed. The man's objections had been too immediate, as if his response to Harry's request was childishly obvious. Worse than that, Harry had the impression that Tom didn't think much of him; there just wasn't anything specific that he could put his finger on.

They wandered around the stands, starting with the Household Cavalry and Army aviation. The only one relatively quiet was the women's military tent. Amused, Julian ran his hand along the side of a Saladin tank on display.

As Harry was patting the heads of two placid Alsatians in the Royal Military Police tent, he heard his name called. He looked up and was surprised to see his wife in front of him. He was about to ask if the boys were with her, but then they raced up and stopped abruptly in front of him.

"Hello, Uncle Harry!" they sang.

Harry introduced Julian to his wife and the boys shook Julian's hand before racing off again. Bridget called out after them not to go too far.

"You should have said you were thinking of coming," Harry said, in a harsher tone than he'd intended. "I'd have sorted you and the boys out with some free tickets."

"Oh, that's all right. It was a last-minute thing. How are you keeping?"

Harry was immediately uncomfortable that Julian might pick up on the polite but obvious estrangement between him and his wife.

"I'm good," Harry said, the presence of Julian stopping him from adding that she looked well.

Harry tried to think how long it had been since he and his

wife were out at a social event together. They had attended a funeral a few years before. He noticed her grey hair was turning white at the temples. Are we that old, he wondered?

"I'd better go after the boys," Bridget said, with a tired smile. "Have a nice time, Harry. Good to meet you, Julian."

"Next time, tell me and I'll get you tickets," Harry said.

Aware that Julian was watching, he gave his wife a peck on the cheek. She responded by giving Julian a comedic look of happy astonishment before hurrying after the boys. Harry watched her, a little put out by her display of humour. Did she have to make it so obvious that there was rarely any affection between them? And was the implication that Harry withheld affection she would actually want to receive? That wasn't the case at all. His feelings were jumbled. It was one thing not to hide the rift between them. It was another to make light of it in public. As he and Julian wandered around the stands, Harry reached the conclusion that she had probably been trying to lighten an awkward situation. And it had been extremely awkward. He should have thought to invite them. He was annoyed with himself for not doing so.

Harry continued to keep an eye out for his wife and the boys. Finally, when it appeared there was nothing left to see and no more people to greet, the motorcyclists started to get ready. Julian and Harry positioned themselves behind the cordon.

The riders were spectacular: uniformed men in black suits, white helmets and gauntlets; they rode in finger-four formation, upside down on ladders, and through flame; then they burst through a hoop with the word 'Triumph' written on it. Petrol and exhaust fumes drifted over the crowd. For the last daredevil stunt: a ramp. On the other side of the field: another ramp. A hoop was placed at the centre of the two. While the equipment was being set up, the military bands drummed and marched.

When the motorcycle rider was ready the hoop was set alight with a flourish. On a signal from his superior, the motorcyclist tore full throttle at the ramp and sailed off into the air. Even to the watching crowd, something was wrong: the angle or the height, or perhaps his teammates who had flinched at the take off. He scraped through the hoop, but there was a gasp of horror from the crowd as the bike buckled and plummeted to the ground, crunching into a tangled heap of rider and machine. He's a gonner, Harry thought. The crowd stood shocked as military doctors sprinted towards the rider. Children cried. Harry grabbed a stunned Julian by the shoulder and pulled him towards the press hut.

"Come on. They'll have information on that kid."

Julian followed Harry, who pulled the heavy metal door of the press hut aside and stopped in surprise. Four journalists were paralytic. The red-bearded military press officer was standing on the table, bowing under his weight and gleefully singing 'Onward, Christian Soldiers'. George, tie off and collar undone, was slumped across the table below the singer – running the risk of being trodden on. George peeled his sticky cheek from the table and waved a cigarette at Harry and Julian to indicate he recognised them.

"No prizes for guessing who'll be writing that story," Harry said to Julian.

Ambulance sirens rolled around the castle and George cocked his head.

"Something happened?"

Julian stared at George, who leaned his head back and regarded Julian with unfocused, red-rimmed eyes.

"Don't you fucking judge me, you fucking prick," he hissed.

George laid his head down on the table again.

Harry put a hand on Julian's shoulder and they left the press hut.

"Let's see if some of the motorcyclists will tell us how tricky that manoeuvre is and whether they noticed anything amiss beforehand," Harry said. "I wonder if my wife saw it. That'll give us something to talk about."

Harry knew it was the second false impression Julian had been given about the reasons for the poor state of his marriage. Bridget had jokingly implied she was starved of affection and he'd probably given Julian the impression that he was starved of conversation. He wondered to himself why they acted so strangely oblique. He concluded it was nobody else's business.

Chapter 17

The Welsh Office was busy with people going in and out. It was housed in the Civic Centre, a building of white Portland stone. With its Corinthian entablature, it looked far grander to Harry than Downing Street. Walking towards the building, he recalled the time when Cledwyn Hughes, Secretary of State, told him that the front door was the only modest thing about 10 Downing Street. The Welsh Office had none of its Chippendale chairs and Queen Anne silver candlesticks. Once Harry had reached Idris' office and sat down, he decided to share with the civil servant, word for word, another observation that Cledwyn had made:

"'If there's a hole in the wall at Downing Street, it's covered with a Gainsborough. In the Welsh Office, it's covered with Polyfilla'."

Idris let out a laugh. "As you probably know, we're setting up a Welsh Arts Council, so maybe we too can get rid of the wall filler."

Harry gave him a sympathetic smile. Idris berated the fact that they were chronically understaffed and looked to remain so for a while, even though they were taking over responsibility for other policy areas.

"It's not unusual for new departments to have staffing problems, of course," Idris said. "Civil servants don't like taking a risk in a new office. Present offices are reluctant to let their best men go. What we need are more youngsters. We need to be attractive to Welsh university graduates."

"They don't have that problem in Scotland."

"I know, but we've got a shortage of assistant principals, a shortage of private secretaries for ministers. Scotland have around eight thousand staff and we've got five hundred. We can't come close to offering the same career prospects and flexibility. But enough of that, how did your trip to Fleet Street go?"

"It's not brilliant news," Harry said. "I don't know yet about the Government imposing a rota party. Personally, I'm hopeful. The Lay Off Aberfan campaign is more difficult. I've looked into it, just to see if my friend in Fleet Street was exaggerating. I think he was probably understating the issue. Wilson's fallen out with Cecil King of the *Mirror*. Cecil King wants his own government."

"His own government?"

"Led by Healey. King's proving a real thorn in the side of Labour. He's openly critical of ministers who don't take notice of what his paper has to say. The *Daily Mirror* are always asking for this or that one to be sacked."

"Where's all this come from?" Idris asked. "They were completely behind him in the last two elections."

"Wilson offered to give King a barony. King refused it. He wanted an earldom. But Wilson won't confer any hereditary peerages."

"I've heard rumours, but I thought that's all they were."

"There's more. An even bigger problem on the Lay Off Aberfan campaign is that last year, before they fell out, Wilson made King a director of the National Coal Board. If they were to run a Lay Off Aberfan campaign, King would be accused of trying to protect the NCB."

Idris sat for a while, taking the information in. Harry noticed a book about Aberfan on Idris' desk which he hadn't seen before.

"What's that you're reading?"

"It's a proof copy, but it's good."

Idris passed the manuscript to Harry – *Aberfan: The Story of a Disaster*.

"This is Tony Austin. I know him. He's a feature writer for the *Western Mail*."

"I've got to remind him we need some of the photographs back. I don't know why the *Western Mail* doesn't get him to cover Aberfan on his own. I'm not a big fan of the other guy."

"George?"

"Yes."

"Me neither."

"If you have any influence over that..."

Harry flicked through the pages of the proof and nodded that he'd like to read it. He wondered at the extraordinary influence Idris seemed to think he had. In one way, Idris' faith in his importance was touching, but in another it was shockingly naïve. Closing the book and turning it over in his hands, he wondered why they hadn't approached Tony for support, given the circumstances. Perhaps, Harry thought, Tony didn't have the time to devote to it. Perhaps the book was enough of a contribution for Tony.

"Talking of reading," Harry said, "when is the Civil Defence report out on the lessons of Aberfan?"

"It's not ready yet, I'm afraid. The Home Office have asked us to redraft certain sections. As soon as it's finalised, you'll be the first to know."

"What's wrong with it?"

"Nothing major. I'll keep you posted."

"I look forward to it."

"And I appreciate your efforts, Harry. We may get results through Downing Street."

"If you're really keen on the idea," Harry said, "I don't see why we can't run it from Wales. It makes more sense, if you think about it. We can run it as patriotism."

"Would the Welsh papers go for it?"

"Maybe. I have a real empathy with what the village went through. And, if it comes to it, there are other ways to bury negative stories."

"We can't have a word of this getting out. But perhaps a Welsh campaign could actually work. A response from London is forthcoming. We shouldn't have too long to wait and we'll know exactly where we are."

Harry noted the details and thanked Idris. Despite the civil servant's considerate manner, Harry didn't believe that the meeting had gone well at all. The Welsh Office wanted the Nationals to pick it up. It was written all over Idris' face. He'd hesitantly agreed that a Welsh campaign might work, but without the slightest bit of enthusiasm or real gratitude that Harry was trying to drive the plan forward. That's the problem with Wales, he brooded; people only think a Welsh project or proposal has any value if it's endorsed by England. The more Harry thought about it, the more deeply insulted he became. And the more insulted he was, the more his determination and confidence returned. It was a sort of backhanded comfort. Wales isn't entirely powerless, Harry thought. He knew he had some clout, but it was getting others to put their faith in him. He sighed and rubbed his forehead with the palm of his hand. A group of students laughed as they went past. Laughter. How silent everything had been that day. Over one hundred school children and not a sound.

Harry marched back from the Welsh Office with a fighting step that would have been admired at the Searchlight Tattoo. He was still deep in thought when he returned to the newsroom, and he was surprised at how out of breath he was after his hot-tempered walk and having climbed the stairs. He recovered himself and dragged his thoughts from his talk with Idris, focusing on the next story to be written.

Plaid wanted the electoral registration forms in English and Welsh. As it stood, they were distributed in Cardiff only in English. Idris had provided a helpful explanation before Harry left. At least this article would remind Cardiff that if they wanted Welsh forms, they only had to ask. Cledwyn would be happy. Increasing nationalism served as a good excuse for the Welsh Office to take on more powers. Harry placed his fingers on the keys of the battered typewriter and let his wrists rest on the lower letters. How old his hands looked. The late evening sunshine pouring through the windows of Thomson House had turned them gold-pink, but they were reddish and dry around the knuckles – a hint of green in the herringbone patterns of his old veins. He flexed his fingers and turned his hands over, noting the delicate cresting waves and whorls of his fingerprints – the smudge of news ink on his thumb. He rested his hands on the keys. There was another story to get out. He could think of Aberfan after he got going. Slowly, he began putting pressure on the metal stalks, hearing the satisfying punch of the hammer strike.

Once the story was written, Harry looked across at Julian's seat. He hadn't seen anyone in the office all day. He dropped his copy in the subs' tray and packed up. He would forgo his usual trip to the pub. A rather annoying council worker had started turning up and Harry found it difficult to avoid getting lumbered with him unless he was downright rude. He could have had a drink elsewhere, but he wasn't in the right frame of mind.

He needed to think.

Chapter 18

"There's been a murder. You need to get down here right now."

"What?" Harry said to the familiar voice.

"Get down here!"

"Where?"

"Across the road from me."

Harry had anticipated a dull day. He had arrived at work early and things were quiet. The smell of the newsroom was very different in the early morning. It was stronger – stale tobacco, sweat, subs' glue and the unsavoury sweetness of fresh newspaper. Harry had even allowed himself a few moments to contemplate the shifting shadows, absorb the quiet and take in the overwhelming mess. The building hadn't been entirely empty when he'd arrived. Winfields' cleaning girls were in, and below, in the print room, a group of workers were setting up, but little of their noise filtered upstairs.

Harry had done some housekeeping and peeled his Aberfan clippings from the wall, placing them flat inside a paper folder. Many of them had gone up on the day of the disaster. When he was finished, he realised how much tidier his desk looked. Rifling through his recent stack of *Echo* newspapers, he found the story about the *Ulysses* ban. He cut it out and taped it to his wall. With it, he pasted up his splash about Doxsey's corruption.

It was such a shame that his Fleet Street enquiries had come to so little. As the hubbub of the newsroom increased and everyone became consumed with their own stories or circulation, he wondered how much good he could do on his own. He remembered once again feeling impotent against the tides of journalists who flowed towards the tip. He had to hold onto that anger. He focused on recalling Idris' uncertain but polite face when he had mentioned that the Lay Off Aberfan campaign should be Welsh. His phone rang and he snatched it up as though it might have someone from England on the other end, wanting to tell Harry they were better than him.

"Harry Roberts," he snapped, only to have Glyn give him the news that made his pulse quicken with excitement.

Harry pulled his coat on, and fumbling with his sleeves in haste, he motioned for Julian to get ready to follow him. As Julian drove, he absorbed the history of Harry's friendship with Glyn and listened out for his colleague's occasional directions. The windscreen wipers squeaked and an autumn leaf lodged itself under one of the blades.

"I've known Glyn for a couple of years," Harry said. "First time I met him, he'd come into the front office but no one would see him. His wife had run off after they had this awful row. He wanted me to put an appeal in the paper. It was a quiet day for news, so I wrote the appeal and she came back the next day. Now, she probably didn't even see it. My guess is she talked to a friend or a neighbour and she calmed down on her own.

"And he's grateful."

"He insists I saved his marriage."

Julian thought that Harry's ongoing friendship with Glyn was a nice thing and said so.

"There's another story I ought to tell you."

"I'm listening."

"A few years after leaving Fleet Street and joining the *Echo*, I did this other story about a heartbroken husband. His wife had accidentally overdosed on a new contraceptive pill. I was at the inquest."

"I've heard of tragedies like that happening."

"Yes, but the widower started badgering me. He was never satisfied – wanted endless coverage. I avoided him and dodged his calls. I suspected he was trying to bolster his claim for compensation or something."

"How did you get rid of him?"

"I wish I hadn't. One day the Coroner's Office called to tell me he'd gassed himself in his car. On the passenger seat, he'd left his wedding album and three letters – one for the police, one for his mother, and one for me. He thanked me in it – for my help. It haunted me for a long time. What help had I given? Very bloody little! By the time Glyn contacted me about his wife, I was a less cynical reporter."

Julian pulled up. The wet street shone. A parked panda car's blue light was on, but it was out-dazzled by the sunlight which flashed and sparkled off the mirrors, wet roof and silver bumper. Two veteran police officers, both with military bearing and chinstraps grazing their bottom lips, stood to attention outside a rundown terrace house. Interested residents had formed into two groups. Each was comprised mostly of women. An ambulance was parked further down. On the left side of the street, Glyn stood in a doorway and motioned the journalists over.

"Come in. Come in!"

Harry introduced Julian and then got his notebook and pen ready. Glyn led them through the house into a messy kitchen. Once there, he stood with his back to the sink and motioned for them to sit at a small table covered with a burnt oilcloth. There was a strong smell of tea and boiled vegetables. There was also the customary dresser, Belfast sink and black iron stove. The floor was linoleum and cotton matting, and the walls were decorated with an odd fruit-and-vegetable wallpaper.

"What a day I've had," Glyn said, "but I might just have something to pay you back, Harry."

"You know there's no need."

"I think you'll like this."

"Yeah?"

"It was me that found the body. I was coming home from the steelworks and there was a woman coming down the road covered in blood. I thought she'd been in an accident or something, so I asked her if she needed help, but she pointed indoors and said she'd done it. I ran in and there was no one downstairs, so up I raced. There was blood on the banister, see. When I went into the bedroom there was a woman's body in the bed. She'd been stabbed. It was her sister that did it and the knife was on the floor. I called the police."

Glyn explained that the women were known prostitutes and had fallen out some months before. Julian and Harry exchanged a look. This was going to be front page: a sensational story.

"I've kept it in there," Glyn said, motioning to the living room.

"Kept what?" Harry said. "Tell me you didn't take the knife."

"No, no, no. Of course not. I left that for the police."

"So what...?"

"The baby."

"The baby?" Harry said, standing up. "What baby?"

"There was a baby in the bed. Covered in blood. I didn't want to leave it there. I thought you might come down so I kept it for you."

As if on cue, an infant began to wail. The three men entered the front room to find Glyn's wife cradling the child. Harry approached them and leant over, his expression one of surprise and pity.

"Good God," Harry whispered.

"We've cleaned her up," Glyn's wife explained, lifting the infant towards Harry. "A little girl. What a start in life. Poor thing."

"Have you told the police?" Harry said, running a finger tenderly from the child's temple to her chin. He could hear the murmur of discussions growing louder across the road.

"Like I said, I kept it for you. I thought you might come down. Maybe your Bridget could take care of it?"

"Okay, Glyn." Harry exhaled out of exasperation and tried to be patient. "Thank you. I'll just have a word with the police and explain."

The two journalists left Glyn and his wife with the baby and headed over to the murder scene.

"I can't believe him," Julian said. "Why didn't he tell them straight away?"

"It's an incredible story."

"Didn't you ever want kids, Harry?"

Too excited to respond to such a personal question, Harry formed the shape of the *Echo* headline in the air. "I can see the front page now: 'Harry Roberts, our own journalist, found the baby'." He stopped dead in his tracks. "Shit. It's Sergeant Jenkins. Nasty bastard. Watch yourself."

"Morning," the sergeant said through gritted teeth.

"Morning. Uh. Nasty business," Harry said, pointing a thumb in the direction of the open door.

"Hmm."

"Do you know there's a baby?"

The sergeant's eyes narrowed as he took a step closer to Harry and forced him back.

"What do you mean that 'there's a baby'?" he said, closing the distance again.

The mothers in the street crowded around them, fascinated.

"The chap who found the body didn't want to leave the child there."

"Stupid bloody bastard! Where is he?"

Julian and Harry hurried after the furious sergeant, who had begun to break out in hives. The mothers followed and the children skipped about until one bumped into Harry and was slapped on the ear by his mother.

"He was waiting for me to arrive," Harry said.

"You're interfering with our investigation!"

"I didn't ask him to do it."

"Fucking journalists."

The sergeant stopped and issued a vicious kick from nowhere which missed Harry and caught Julian on the side of his left shin. Julian let out an involuntary yelp and doubled over. He hobbled out of kicking range and pulled up his trouser leg to examine the painful injury. It was already bluish purple and bleeding.

"You brute!" said one of the mothers. "There was no need for that."

"Mind your own business," the sergeant snapped.

"You should be out catching criminals – not kicking innocent bystanders."

The mothers fussed over Julian until they heard the baby's cries coming from Glyn's house. They soon forgot all about him and gathered around the front window, cooing and clucking in sympathy.

The sergeant stepped to kick Harry, who jumped out the way.

"He's at it again," one of the women screamed. "Someone should report him."

"If you're here when I come back out, I'm going to call the van."

No one was sure if the sergeant was addressing the journalists or the women who'd been denouncing his violence, so everyone backed away. The women crossed the road and returned to their huddles outside the scene of the crime. Julian limped back to his car with Harry, not comforted in the least by the older journalist's amusement.

As he started the car, Julian watched in his rear-view mirror as Sergeant Jenkins exited the house with the screaming baby in his arms. The sergeant then turned and glared up the road after them.

While writing up the story of the murder and rescued baby, Harry took another call. This time he shooed Julian out of earshot. It was Idris again, asking him to return to the Welsh Office as soon as he had time. When the story was complete, Harry escaped Thomson House for the Civic Centre.

The old man was animated. Something had changed in the few days since they'd met and Harry could sense good news. Were things gathering pace? Harry had mixed feelings about this. What if Downing Street had given the Lay Off Aberfan campaign to the *Mirror*, despite all indications otherwise? Idris waved Harry to sit down.

"Mr Marshall confirms to me that things have been exacerbated somewhat by some civic leaders basking, so to speak, in the publicity that has come out of Aberfan: enjoying a certain notoriety. But he believes the day of reckoning has come."

Harry nodded, thinking that this basking in publicity wasn't restricted to civic leaders.

"It should have been taken care of at the outset."

"They tried, Harry. My colleague, Paul Marshall, tried to take charge himself. He told Selwyn Jones that he could help them manage the publicity, but things moved too fast. There was no time to put a publicity policy together. And someone else is back in Aberfan."

"Who?"

"That journalist you had the falling out with. Falstone?"

"He's back?"

"We think it's him. He's one of many, in any event."

Harry rubbed the bridge of his nose, unable to think of anything to say.

"We're trying to deal with it diplomatically. That trip to London..."

"Fleet Street?"

"No, no, no," Idris said. "The parents' trip."

"The...?"

"Coach load of parents from Aberfan, supposedly going to throw slag at..."

"Ah, Number 10. Right. I get you."

"The coach reached London, but the threat wasn't carried out. It was a setup. Whichever member of the press was behind it, they failed to rouse the numbers from Aberfan and had to cajole people along from surrounding villages."

Harry wondered how much worse it could get.

"And do you remember that I asked you about Mr Edwards?" Idris continued.

"Yes? I was wondering about that."

"Some low-life freelancer realised the Press Association weren't buying the spurious stories so they incited a couple of fathers, Edwards and Bridges, first to corroborate the stories and, when that failed, to phone PA directly. PA had used a couple of the stories, but when they finally checked the information, they found it to be incorrect. Then about a month ago, for example, Edwards and Bridges, encouraged by the press, organised a protest march. Fortunately, they were the only ones to turn up."

"The rest of the villagers took no notice? That's good."

"But whoever is pulling the strings with Edwards and Bridges didn't give up. On August thirtieth, the two men succeeded in persuading fifty parents to turn up to a local meeting. S O Davies is talking about evil press influences going on in the village."

"But what can we do?" Harry asked.

"I wonder if I could quote you in a follow-up letter to the Press Secretary? I want to tell him that I am in casual talks with bona fide journalists and that you are also extremely worried. I'd like to also tell him that there are journalists who refuse to take on board potentially malicious stories and have tried to discourage others from doing so. I'm going to bring in Cliff Phillips. You probably know him. Press Association?"

"Yes, I know him well. He's a good man. I was at his wedding."

"Another idea is that the Secretary of State could issue a statement to the press and television, asking for a restriction of coverage as a mark of respect. He's off to America, of course, so he'll have to do it before he goes, but that shouldn't be a problem. We'll also get a minister from the Welsh Office to attend the memorial service. There are also the enormous number of messages from well-wishers – on a global scale – which are going to be received in Merthyr in mid to late October. It'll be a repeat of last year, messages from priests, parents, teachers, classes of children and miners. We even received a letter from Maitland, an Australian coalmining community, after they lost five workers in an accident themselves on the very day of the disaster."

Harry felt an urge to say something meaningful about the human cost of mining, but the subject was too big to be summed up in a sentence or two. Idris moved on:

"These messages will be managed in two or three press conferences and we can handle the way they're delivered. It will be hard news only. We'll talk about the source and the number of messages and avoid reading the messages themselves."

"Makes sense."

"And we'll certainly have to avoid any reference to the fact that the Kray twins have donated more than any individual so far: one hundred pounds. Granted, there's two of them, but that's not the point. Can you imagine Fleet Street with that one?"

There was a knock at the civil servant's door, which opened without invitation from Idris. He merely smiled and stood. A stout woman entered backwards wheeling a trolley with a pot of tea, cups, a jug of water and a plate of biscuits. Idris suggested a break as they still had a number of things to cover and he didn't want to exhaust the journalist by overloading him. Idris tried to keep the talk away from Aberfan, but Harry was unable to leave it alone. The journalist pressed for any details that the civil servant might have about plans for the anniversary.

"Ah," Idris said, giving in as he noisily poured the tea. "The only thing we know that's in the pipeline for certain is that the BBC plan to produce a special programme. Now, I hear from the Town Clerk that they have agreed to a prior showing of the film to the people of Aberfan. What does that tell you?"

Idris handed Harry his tea and waited for an answer.

"They're nervous."

"Exactly. The BBC spent a great deal of time filming and interviewing the psychiatrists working with the bereaved. We'll see what happens when the film is shown, but it could be that it's controversial. If Downing Street approached the Nationals about a limited and dignified coverage of Aberfan during the anniversary period, then the BBC would be morally bound to drop their film."

"That'll cost them."

"They'll have little choice. I'm assuming your lot are already laying down plans for anniversary coverage and we can assume every newspaper office in the country is doing likewise. We're looking into creating some sort of official lead – but if this doesn't happen, I think we can expect the popular press to go to town with flash pictures."

Idris clenched his fists repeatedly as though he had a problem with circulation and put his left elbow on the desk. He pursed his mouth against the knuckles of his left hand, seeming to think for a moment about what was next on the agenda.

"And one memorial service is hard enough to control. Now we've got two."

"How's that?"

"The Parents' Association want the memorial service in the cemetery to take place on the anniversary of the funerals rather than the disaster. Understandable, but it has the unfortunate side effect of putting the village in the spotlight for at least a week. The anniversary is on the twenty-first and the memorial service is on the twenty-seventh. Added to which, there'll be Continental and North American newsmen sent to Aberfan on 'One Year On' assignments. I know I keep talking about Wales' image – and that's vitally important, all those deeply upsetting pictures in the paper, but it's Aberfan who are going to feel it most."

Harry asked Idris if anyone had canvassed the village for what they might tolerate in terms of publicity.

"It's all a bit vague," Idris replied. "They're not really thinking about it. Perhaps they're not expecting it to be as overwhelming as we imagine it will be. But here's a thought I had this morning. We're talking about a village in receipt of widespread psychiatric treatment to help them over the trauma. Perhaps it's too much for them to think of?"

"You're suggesting they're not thinking clearly?"

"Yes. No. I'm not sure. But think about it. At the time, when the press were all over them, they were too distressed to notice fully. And rightly so. But this time, they're going to be more aware. The only motivation of a lot of these journalists is to capture the most poignant picture or get the saddest anniversary story. They'll write nothing about how the villagers have been brave and courageous in such dark circumstances or how the community has come together."

"This is a disaster. It's all been left too late to manage."

"Let's not be too gloomy. The Lay Off Aberfan campaign may work yet if it's taken up at Downing Street's end. And I've had a lengthy conversation with Trevor Lloyd-Hughes. That's why I brought you in. Expect all this to be put into action, because he's certainly aware of the seriousness of the situation. He sounded in a positively fighting spirit over it. Said he'd speak to Wilson as soon as possible about what the Government can offer."

Idris drew to a halt and reflected. He looked at his list and followed down the items with a pen, pausing to ensure he hadn't missed anything.

"Do you have any questions, Harry?"

"How long have you been keeping tabs on Falstone?"

"Forget it for now."

Harry bowed. More fool the *Mirror*, he thought. The Lay Off Aberfan campaign was his project and he was going to speak for Wales in a way he never ordinarily could as a journalist. And the meeting had cleared up a particular worry of Harry's in respect of timing. The fact that there were two services was a real bonus. It might be possible, with two dates, to restrict press coverage of the anniversary itself and then spend the following week spreading word of the Lay Off Aberfan campaign in readiness. Cheering up, Harry considered that his efforts might even have an influence on the way news was reported in the future.

Chapter 19

Almost a full year on from Aberfan, Harry arrived home after a long day at work and was still trying hard to ignore the fact that he'd turned sixty-one that morning.

If Harry had any birthday wish, it was that George would get his comeuppance, not least because Harry had heard him more than once that day claim to have arrived at Aberfan first. The wish had come to mind as he picked up three birthday cards lying on the doormat. Harry didn't open the cards immediately. He knew they were from his two sisters and sister-in-law. He ran his hands around the edges of the white envelopes as though he were about to shuffle a deck of playing cards and propped them up on the mantelpiece where a few other unopened letters were stacked. If he guessed at unurgent contents, he didn't trouble himself to open mail right away. These days, there were few surprises.

The rivalry between himself and George was a major headache for Harry now that he wanted to exert some control over the paper regarding Aberfan publicity. An outsider might have thought that sister papers produced in the same room shared a camaraderie, but the newspapers competed for popularity and had never been anything other than rivals divided by the subs' desk. Both had their own signature style. The *Western Mail* was a wordy establishment broadsheet, stuffier and more business-minded. The *Echo* tried for a mass appeal with simple, blocky sans serif headlines.

Harry found a couple of sheets of plain paper and took his dusty, blue Olivetti Underwood typewriter out from the cupboard under the stairs. He hadn't used it in years. He examined the paper front and back to make sure there was nothing which might give him away. If Harry's cunning idea worked, even George would have to pretend he was happy with the outcome. Harry rolled the paper into the machine and typed a badly written letter complaining that George's reporting on Aberfan was both disrespectful and sloppy. The fact that Harry was unused to typing on the Underwood naturally produced a few spelling mistakes. He also brought up the fact that there had been spelling errors in George's writing, which there had been, including such instances as 'The Aberfan Traged', although the blame could only be laid at the door of proofing or printing. He signed it, 'A Reader'.

Happy with his work, he pulled the sheet out and typed a similar letter from a Mr N Hughes. He'd keep sending these letters in and see what came of it. He searched through the bureau and found what he was looking for. Bridget's leather stationery holder was full of thick cream envelopes a man like Harry would never ordinarily use.

He jumped as a key turned in the front door but realised it was Bridget. She tended to come and go as she pleased. When she visited it was as though she had never left. She was at home still, in what was now his home. Bridget placed a white confectionary box on the polished coffee table, kissed him on the head and peeked to see what he was typing.

"Happy Birthday, dear. Did you have a good day?"

"Not bad, love. Thanks."

"Readers' letters, is it? You haven't done that in a while."

Bridget stood for a moment before smoothing the back of her skirt and sitting neatly on the chair opposite.

"Want a cup of tea?" Harry asked.

"No thanks. Just popped in to wish you well. See if you needed anything."

"How's your sister?"

"She's fine. Did you get her card?"

"Thank her for me. How are the kids?"

Harry looked at his unopened cards and then at Bridget, who was sat in shadow. She leaned over the side of the chair and fumbled, looking for the lamp switch. Her hair had been getting shorter and wavier over the years. Definitely whiter. She was broad round the middle, but her legs were trim. Her hands were crossed in her lap, left in right, palms up, her thumbs locked together as though she was about to make the shadow of a bird on the wall. He missed her, prickly though she was at times. He knew it would be a mistake to persuade her to try again if he didn't have the time for her. Bridget pressed down both palms on her legs and stood up, noting that Harry had returned to reading over his typing.

"Did you enjoy the Tattoo?"

"Sorry?"

Harry stopped typing and looked up.

"The Tattoo?" she repeated.

"I would have invited you."

"Why didn't you?"

Harry was annoyed, but that was Bridget's way sometimes. She'd say something pointed or confrontational, but if he reacted badly she would dismiss it as a joke. Then she would immediately stop teasing him and sulk about him being moody. Harry returned his gaze to his typing but nodded in her direction that his oversight had been noted.

Bridget kissed him on the head before she left, and he gently wrapped his fingers around her wrist for a second without looking up. It was a gesture that was meant to say that she should be patient. He had no idea whether she understood it or not. Feeling a pang of guilt, he jumped up and followed her to the door to help with her coat. He stood in the doorway and watched her head down the street until she turned the corner. The lights were on in the church opposite, illuminating the stained-glass saints. He made out one or two stars twinkling behind a thin veil of night-time clouds.

They'd married at St Albans and not once had they considered that children might not happen. They only concerned themselves with wondering when to decorate the spare room and how they would manage financially. Harry, wanting a few selfish years of married life first, had never considered that this natural longing would be denied. They were Catholic. They were young and healthy. Bridget had planned and expected. Month after month she was disappointed, only to have her hopes rise again. Initially, she consulted her doctor. She was told to relax and let nature take its course. The priests, guessing at her wishes, told her to pray.

Harry had been determined to be a different kind of father from his own. Not that his old man had been all bad. He'd simply been absent – war, or at work in the Cardiff Docks office, or grunting and coughing behind the *Cardiff Times*. Harry had things to share with his children. He had vaguely romantic notions that his boy – or girl for that matter, though it was always a boy he imagined – would follow him into the news industry.

Childless years had followed, where Bridget chattered and laughed about it constantly as if talk might somehow bear fruit. She had a seemingly endless narrative of boys' names, girls' names, preferred schools, friends their children would have of the same age, behaviour she would allow and behaviour she would not. She took a keen interest in childrearing and discipline. Then the questions had come. Do you think there's a problem? With me? With you? With us? Her friends getting pregnant had been hard for her. Harry considered with hindsight that talking about it incessantly might have been for their benefit rather than her own. Who knew?

Then came the war. A respite from that nagging question of 'When?' Babies were born during the war, of course, but Harry and Bridget were separated and the pressure was off. At thirty-three he was on the old side, but they wanted journalists. By the time the war was over, Harry, age thirty-nine, was reluctant to return to this unending battle on the home front. He longed for peace. He wanted Bridget to talk about something – anything – else.

When Bridget demanded he make love to her, the paradox was that he couldn't think of anything he would rather do less. He threw himself into his work and was never short of an excuse to avoid returning home. He told himself that he would make her happy by working hard. It was a shame, he thought, that his wife was not more materialistic. A living room full of Stag furniture was testimony to that. She polished it every day, of course, but he couldn't say it brought her much consolation.

Two operations followed. It had been her in the end. It was fine to say no one was to blame, but he had absorbed the blame for so long that he was happy to have the responsibility removed from his shoulders. Sadly, the surgeries had not been successful. The doctors admitted defeat. For Harry and his wife, there would be no milk and bedtime stories. He thought about Glyn's recent offer. It hadn't been the first time. There had been a family two doors down with far too many children and the mother had promised Bridget the next one she had. After the birth, the mother sent her eldest child down with a message for Bridget to collect the baby if she wanted it. Harry had sent her packing.

Something had changed in Bridget after she reached her late forties. It took him months to realise that her attendance at church had increased significantly, to most days plus helping out with Sunday School and Brownies. She was a devoted Tawny Owl. Endlessly running her fingers over her grandmother's turquoise rosary, she became calmer and resigned. She appeared to have achieved some measure of peace from her business. When he couldn't bear speculating about it any longer, he asked her what had changed. She said it was what God wanted and there were plenty of children in the world. She had been talking to a priest about her predicament. Harry realised later he had, in a way, dealt with the problem in the same way his father dealt with things: behind a newspaper. But at least his father only had the daily edition – he hadn't put the whole bloody news industry between them. Harry wasn't sure if he had wanted her to be nice and reasonable about it. He didn't like that she had surrendered, and he felt a measure of resentment that she had turned to someone else for rescue.

His heightened feelings of sympathy and sudden impulse to make it up to Bridget made her seem more attractive to him. He felt perhaps he could approach her sexually again and saw her in the light he once had: soft, caring and still pretty. Perhaps they could fashion out a nice, childless life for themselves, count their blessings, pretend that there had been a measure of choice in it. Harry was soon put in his place when he remembered her feigning headaches. At first he had thought it was just a matter of time, but it seemed that in accepting she had also moved on.

She wasn't all right about it, anyway. Bridget fussed too much over other children for that to be true. She spoiled her sister's kids rotten; knitted for them constantly and gave them comics and pocket money which her sister didn't know about. She kept a growing trust account for the pair of them in the Post Office. She had a sweetie jar with liquorice allsorts, Black Jacks, Fruit Salads, humbugs and sherbet lemons. They were fed fingers of fudge, lemonade and ice cream. When Bridget had been told off by her sister about her nephews' cavities, Bridget retorted that her sister was too strict on them. The response had been acerbic. Bridget didn't have any children so she had no right to pitch in with her opinion. That night, Harry had arrived home to find his wife distraught, curled on the sofa in the dark. He wrapped himself around her, glad the darkness hid his own eyes' bright tears. It had been years since she had cried like that. It took her and her sister months to patch it up. She'd had to, for their nephews' sake and her own.

If children were the glue that held a family together, then it was hardly surprising that Bridget had eventually gone to live with her sister. It was so horribly ironic that she had turned to God. It was He who refused to give her children, the same deity who was capable of snatching up a school full of them in a single morning.

The planned nursery had eventually been turned into a small library. It was the most charming room in the house but the least inhabited as Harry didn't like reading upstairs. While he did what he liked in terms of organised chaos at work, Bridget had drummed into him early on that he must take care of his possessions. He had stacked his classic books tallest to smallest on a motley collection of shelves and bookcases; their cheerful spines filled the walls with colour. To please Bridget further, Harry had hung up two large pin-and-thread pictures between the freestanding bookshelves. The fashionable artwork had been given to Bridget by her sister. The boys had helped assemble the complicated kits. The nail grids, set into pale blue velvet, geometrically formed the slightly abstract sails of two sailing ships. There was something Harry didn't like about the nail grids and the tightness of the thread. He was pleased to have them out of the way upstairs. In the end, it made little difference to his wife, who showed no interest, save for her initial glassy stare when Harry had told her his plan to give the room its alternative purpose.

Harry, feeling the draught sweeping through the house, closed the front door and stretched forward and back. He carried his birthday cake into the kitchen and waited for the kettle to boil. He cut himself a neat slice and carried his plate and a cup of milky tea back into the living room, where he opened Faulkner's *The Sound and the Fury*, and he lost himself in the words.

Chapter 20

Harry was grateful over the following weeks that he'd had Julian provide him with updates on Doxsey. The trial was set to last a period of sixteen days and had somehow found its way into a packed Magistrates' Court schedule with uncommon speed. As Julian had been involved, and possibly because he was the managing director's nephew, he was chosen as the one who would cover the story from court. Harry would be free to work on the anniversary, oversee the work Julian was doing and carry out some investigative work of his own.

"It's in your hands now, son," Harry said to Julian. "Do me proud."

"But it's your story," Julian insisted.

Harry's thoughts were interrupted by the newsdesk informing him that they'd had a call about another protest march being organised in Aberfan. When Harry asked who had called, he was told it was a Mr Edwards who, as well as organising, was also waiting on a court order application to have the books of the Disaster Fund opened for auditing. Harry had no intention of calling back until he'd thought things through. He took Edwards' number down on a fresh page in his notebook.

When Harry chased it up later, he interrupted Edwards to ask whether he had heard of someone called Falstone. A little put out by the strange question, Edwards assured Harry that he hadn't. Of course he would say that, thought Harry. But he couldn't deny that Mr Edwards had been convincing. Harry thanked him for taking the trouble to call and said that they would be unable to use the story as it was, but if he had anything in the future, he was free to get in touch.

Fortunately for Harry, the newsdesk was busy and appeared

to have forgotten all about the matter. Harry, in the interest of insurance in case they did chase it up, worked hard on three stories and told them that he didn't have time to deal with anything else. He was still jumpy when, as he was about to finish his latest story, Evan called him into his office and told him to shut the door. In the seconds before Harry turned back to the room he prayed that either Evan was considering the Lay Off Aberfan campaign or that he had no suspicions.

"George has been receiving complaints."

Smothering a relieved laugh, Harry mouthed an almost theatrically curious 'O-oh?' as he sat down.

"A couple of readers say that he's not handling Aberfan with the right sensitivity. Steve can't see what the problem is. Neither can I, if I'm honest, but he made the point that if a couple of people are taking the time to write in, there might be many more in agreement who aren't bothering to make their views known. We're looking for a way around it. Steve doesn't want to raise it with George. You know what he's like."

Harry rose, walked behind his chair, placed both hands on the back and faced Evan.

"Maybe I've got an idea."

"What have you got?"

"I don't know if it'll work, but what about serialisation?"

Harry, looking more animated by the second, returned to his seat and put his hands on his knees, pleased.

"Okay?"

"Why don't they serialise Tony's book?"

Evan smiled.

"Publish exclusive extracts in sections," Harry continued. "The public will love it. Tony will sell loads of books. George won't be any the wiser. The *Western Mail* can revise it to fit their content requirements."

"That's not a bad idea, old man."

"I'm full of them."

"Brilliant. Go and get Steve in here."

Harry's first thought was that he deserved a drink. When he finally returned to his desk, he found a large envelope addressed to him. Inside was a sheaf of papers with an unsigned note on top: 'This interesting and potentially useful report is being completely buried by the Welsh Office'.

Someone had leaked him the Civil Defence report that Idris had promised but not delivered. Harry read through the lessons from Aberfan highlighted by General Anderson but failed to find anything particularly contentious. He decided to sit on the report until he could run it by Idris.

Drawn to the soft light, he put the report in his desk drawer and went to the window. Sunset tinted the clouds baby pink against baby blue. He leaned towards the glass and looked up. The head teacher of Pantglas Junior School came to mind again. He only wanted to feel happy and pleased with himself – but there she was – like a shadow.

A few weeks later, Julian was in the overcrowded Cathays Park Law Courts where the Magistrates' were losing a battle for space with the Crown. The Magistrates' had already been forced to use a temporary court miles away to hear domestic and care cases. It was only the seriousness of the Doxsey case and the people involved that meant it was to be heard so soon. Four days into Doxsey's hearing, Harry was walking in that direction as he made his way to the Welsh Office. The peal of the City Hall clock bell drew his eyes as well as his ears towards the courts, where Julian was presumably back in his seat. Once the case and the memorial service were over, he'd really spend some time with the boy.

Harry hurried on, trying to shield himself from the rain storm. For the last few weeks it had done nothing but pour down. Back at the newsroom, socks had been left to dry out in front of electric fires. Cars swished past. Pedestrians dodged spray and tiptoed around puddles prickling like pans of water coming to a boil. Women held umbrellas in both hands like bridal bouquets and the city's parks resembled overused rugby pitches. With the anniversary reminding the Welsh in the Valleys of the fragility of the coal tips, many villagers were starting to raise their worried faces towards the mountains, fearing for their families.

Harry pumped his brolly open a few times to dry it, thankful that it had survived. He jogged into the Welsh Office and waited in the foyer while Idris' secretary announced his arrival. When he saw his friend he knew it was bad news. There was a tension around Idris' mouth, although the words that came out were cordial as ever. Again, Idris slid a letter across to Harry. It was dated the day before, 28 September, from Harold Wilson's Press Secretary, Trevor Lloyd-Hughes. It was the Downing Street letter they'd been waiting for. Harry looked aghast at Idris and then continued reading. The Prime Minister and Trevor were in complete agreement. To offer help would put the Government in a false position. Even if they were to make the gentlest approach to the press, the most cautious and considered gesture would probably make absolutely no difference to the outcome, other than to potentially put the Government into difficulty. They didn't anticipate having any power over the press whatsoever, regardless of whether they approached them diplomatically or waded in with threats.

The Press Secretary's letter echoed the comments Tom had made during Harry's visit to see him at Fleet Street. The Newspaper Publishers' Association had little power. The Government blamed it on poor administration within such organisations, concluding that they had little real influence on their members.

The rota party proposal didn't get more than a sentence in reply. Harry let out a small groan when he reached it. That had been the one idea he thought would have merit with Downing Street. They said they didn't believe any newspaper would agree to rota party coverage. There was no reason given. Lloyd-Hughes asserted that, as the memorial service had been organised by the people of Aberfan, then they were no doubt prepared and expecting press coverage commensurate with the occasion. It was inevitable, he wrote, that the memorial service being organised by the people of Aberfan would be of considerable news interest to the public. For this reason, the reporting of it was to be left to the good taste, and sense of responsibility, possessed by the television and press authorities.

The letter went on to warn that it would put the Government in a very difficult position if Downing Street or the Secretary of State for Wales sought to restrict the coverage or, equally problematic, implied that the press would be distasteful or disrespectful were they to cover the memorial service.

Harry didn't see the problem. It wasn't necessarily disrespectful coverage they were talking about but disrespectful reporters. Downing Street could have easily got the word out that if reporters visited Aberfan, they would need to conduct themselves well or face being referred to the Press Council. Harry wished that he'd been in on this from the start and had the opportunity to contribute to Idris' letter before it was sent. He could have narrowed down the request to a few key suggestions which might have had a chance of succeeding.

What really demonstrated Number 10 were washing their hands of the whole thing was that they believed if the Government showed any anxiety, then they might, by implication, accept responsibility for a disaster which was not theirs. Idris had mentioned that the publicity might be damaging for a decade, and the Prime Minister had therefore raised the point that the Government did not want to set a precedent for managing the Aberfan anniversary and still be saddled with it in ten years' time. Further, Downing Street, if they interfered, would be accused of news management at the very least, incurring the wrath of all the papers. What the paragraph didn't hint at, of course, was that Cecil King would have told Wilson to shove it, regardless.

The Downing Street correspondence concluded by making it clear that the behaviour of the press and coverage of Aberfan was out of their hands and out of their control, but that didn't necessarily mean the actual situation was. The editors of these papers, it was suggested, were not heartless dictators, and it was possible that the Welsh Office and Merthyr Borough Council were getting worked up about a situation that wouldn't be half as bad as they were expecting. Easy for them to say, thought Harry.

"Honestly," Idris said, "it's a complete U-turn from what he said on the phone the other day. I phoned him up again earlier to get to the bottom of it. He apologised and said his hands were tied. He reminded me that Sir Elwyn Jones, the Attorney General, had already got into hot water with the Nationals over Aberfan."

"I remember, I think."

"You must. A number of integral witnesses involved in the Aberfan disaster were being confronted live on air. I'm talking about NCB officials rather than the villagers. Sir Elwyn Jones warned the press not to cross-examine witnesses because it might, of course, have a bearing on Edmund Davies' inquiry. The Nationals went crazy, claiming fascism had taken over. Sir Elwyn Jones was lampooned in Fleet Street cartoons wearing a Hitler moustache."

"Did they say anything specific about the *Mirror*?"

"Downing Street took flak when Harold Wilson made Cecil King a director of the National Coal Board in the first place. People said there was a conflict of interest. You can imagine what rival papers are going to say if a newspaper, run by a director of the NCB, leads a campaign to stop publicity about a disaster caused by the NCB themselves."

"Strike that off our list, then," Harry agreed.

"And you know you told me that Cecil King is dreaming of masterminding a political coup?"

"Yes. Led by Healey."

"Not just Healey. Cecil King wants Robens in his new government, too. He's apparently made his views on Robens clear. Did you read the *Mirror* today?"

Harry had. They had run a story claiming Alf Robens should carry on with the fine job he's doing at the Coal Board.

"What I'm really annoyed about is that Trevor Lloyd-Hughes didn't give me a clue. If he had an idea it was going to go this way, he should have used more caution. I'd have seen it coming. I had every confidence that Downing Street were going to help. Peter Marshall and I are now prevented from helping Merthyr. It's the worst-case scenario. If we go against Downing Street, the Welsh Office might find itself opposed by Parliament in the future."

"You should have come to me sooner. I got a complete overview of the political situation just by talking to Tom Powell from the *Express*."

"I couldn't agree more, with hindsight, but I was advised not to bring anyone in at all. What we really need to focus on is where we go from here."

Idris was silent for a minute or two, downcast and pondering his own question.

"What are you going to say to Merthyr?" Harry asked.

"I'll have to be careful. They've appealed to us for help and I'll have to tell them no. Someone will no doubt appeal to you to write about the failure of our proposals. And I suppose that's an end to the matter, apart from..."

"What?"

"Nothing."

"What if I were to persuade Evan to run the campaign?"

"A drop in the ocean. And from what it sounds like, it would be down to the editor in chief."

"It's better than kowtowing to England – the politicians and the press. They're the problem."

"And what's your solution?"

"We need more than your collective letters of complaint to

England. We need to do something more. To every action, there is an equal and opposite reaction."

Somewhere in the back of Harry's mind, he was aware that he might be giving Idris the impression he was desperate to stay involved. He dismissed this, thinking that Idris had displayed his own desperation by involving him in the first place, and that such a candid, impassioned offer – which obviously went against journalistic ethics – might well show Idris what a true friend he had in Harry, what true solidarity he represented. And he wasn't finished.

"Idris, I found this on my chair in Thomson House."

Harry took the Civil Defence report out from the folds of his coat and placed it on Idris' desk. Idris was silent for a moment as he scanned the document.

"When?" Idris said.

"About three weeks ago."

"Where the hell did you get it?"

"As I said, it was on my chair."

"Did you find out who left it?"

"It would have been left at the front desk, Idris. I have no idea."

"Just wait until I find the bloody person responsible."

"Let's not have a witch-hunt. You were going to show it to me anyway, remember?"

"I was wrong to tell you that, Harry. We were wrong to commission the bloody thing in the first place."

"It's helpful."

"Oh yes, there are plenty of good tips for the future: the passes and permits to deter sightseers, perhaps a broadcast asking the public to stay away; suitable headquarters for disaster operations to be identified by councils beforehand, so they'll have all the right facilities rather than taking over every poorly equipped chapel and cinema; and raising general awareness that people can behave irrationally during disasters. All useful."

Harry, who had been staring at the floor while listening, looked sharply at Idris. The mention of both the cinema and people acting irrationally made him shift uncomfortably.

"So why bury it?" Harry asked.

"We haven't completely. A handful of clerks from the various counties have it – strictly confidential. We found the report too generic – unreliable, even."

Harry sensed there was more and waited.

"Off the record," Idris said, "we were hoping there might be useful advice for others when it comes to future disasters, including how to handle the press, but it's the opposite. The report itself could encourage a media Aberfan post-mortem on whatever shortcomings the rescue services had."

Harry imagined himself receiving the report as a Fleet Street journalist and how differently he would have treated the story and the report itself.

"I get it, Idris. I also understand you're annoyed it's been leaked, but I want you to promise me there won't be a witch-hunt. There's no damage done. Let's not get distracted from the big picture."

"I was never worried about the *Echo*. I know you were always going to handle it sensitively."

Harry frowned, concerned that this was not the response hoped for.

"It's worth thinking further about," Harry went on. "But I'm the only one left who can try and control this thing."

"Your editor will never go for it."

"We haven't run a campaign in ages."

"This is all off the record, you know."

"Of course."

"And no one is to find out about this."

"No one.

Chapter 21

Harry had visited the Taff the way someone might visit a sick relative. For five minutes of his lunch he had stood on the bridge and stared down at it sympathetically. The river levels had risen with continual rain and black clouds had rolled across the sky like a coal train, but the colour of the water hadn't changed.

Back at work and on the phone, the Glamorgan River Authority was starting to sound more and more like a medical consultant.

"What's the prognosis?" Harry asked them.

The prognosis was bad. Harry had to work hard to spin the story in the right direction. He talked the man on the phone around in circles until he admitted, reluctantly, that the Taff might be clean in months. The actual time period was one to two years, but Harry assured him he would not put such specifics in his story.

"There are four weirs on the Taff," the contact said, encouraged by Harry's optimism. "They take care of reaeration. They get oxygen back into the water. And the Taff is a steep river, which also helps with oxygen levels. It can take care of itself, if we stop chucking pollutants into it. It all depends on how quickly the NCB can stabilise the tips and how soon we can improve sewerage treatment."

Satisfied with the piece, Harry knocked off early to get ready for choir. He had looked forward to it all day. The music made things clearer, as did walking. It sharpened his thoughts, especially when they sang something well known, so that while one part of him sang automatically, another part opened up. It was almost like dowsing or water divining his own feelings. The music pulled out of him a deep desire to stand up for Wales, and he would always try his best to remember these passions and take them with him. But although the music gave Harry determination, he knew from experience that it was ephemeral. Once the rehearsal was over, normality would return. It was a case of enjoying the feeling while it lasted. He dearly wished that such reassurances would linger, but they always began to fade before he left the hall, and any dim phrases he clung to would be washed away by the din of the city.

But that night after choir, in spite of Harry's protestations and very real tiredness, he found himself pressganged to the pub to talk about yet another problem the Welsh Office were having with the press. His patriotism and sense of importance grew as the old boys made a fuss of him. He was pushed and carried into the pub by the weight of their enthusiasm. Once they were settled around a table, they all, including Harry, looked to Idris to explain.

"We had a meeting last night," Idris began. "S O Davies is under constant pressure from press and TV to release the design of the memorial at Aberfan. He's worried. If we don't release the design, then the press will find another way to get hold of it."

"You mean they'll go after the village?"

"Precisely. The design was the choice of the parents so it stands to reason if the press get desperate... and work has started on the memorial site for the first stage so it's hard to keep press interest away. We're giving you the details first. It's embargoed until next week, but we trust that you'll do a nice feature for us. S O Davies will be available for interview any time you like. I've told him to expect your call."

They handed Harry a package of information in a brown envelope, together with a sketch of the design. Harry examined the contents, noted the drawing and murmured appreciatively. It would certainly give him plenty for the next day and the BBC would no doubt come calling after they read it.

"The memorial will be a permanent structure and contain

the messages of what Wales, and particularly Aberfan, consider appropriate. It's light marble, so it'll be visible from the Merthyr to Cardiff road. And there will be a plateau. We're particularly pleased with that."

An elderly Welsh Office civil servant with badly fitting false teeth, which he clicked in and out of position, pointed to the plateaued area on the plan.

"That part of the memorial will be finished by the anniversary. The build is in two stages. The first is a walled garden at the far end with a shelter and some seats. Stage two includes rows of arches behind the graves with sculptured motives and a front wall with inset plaques. There'll also be an incumbent cross adjacent to the garden. We anticipate all work being finished by January or February."

The next day was a Friday, and at half past five, having prepared most of his article on the memorial design and knocking out three small local stories, Harry decided to try and convert Evan again. He knocked on the editor's door and took a seat. Evan was dressed in black tie and preparing to leave the office.

"Where are you off?" Harry asked.

"Business Club. Professor Parkinson is giving a lecture on why Wales needs its own government."

"Sounds interesting."

"I'll tell you about it tomorrow. What do you want, anyway?"

"I wonder if you've given any thought to the Lay Off Aberfan campaign."

"How about this. I'll lay you off if you mention it again."

Evan made a face as he sat back down. As if to put some distance between himself and Harry's topic of conversation, he rocked his chair back on two legs and held himself in place by holding onto the front of his desk. The movement knocked two tiny, paper-dry leaves from the bonsai onto his desk. Evan looked at them and raised his eyes to meet Harry's. Evan let his chair fall back on four legs, as if he was ready to talk.

"Let's have a drink," he said.

Surprised, Harry watched Evan as he produced a bottle of Scotch and two glasses. He filled them with generous measure and slid one across.

"A newspaper should never campaign for something they can't win," the editor reminded the old journalist.

"But we might win. And even if we don't, we've shown where we ethically stand." Harry swallowed half his Scotch, appreciating the heat in the back of his throat. "Thank you," he said hoarsely, putting his glass on the desk.

"Ethically? We're a bloody newspaper. We publish news. And what's news? Events are news. And what was the Aberfan disaster? An event. A horrible, catastrophic event. And what is the memorial service? An event in Welsh history. And you want us to not only refuse to report it, but discourage the news industry as a whole from writing about it?"

Harry pursed his lips and got up to leave.

"Sit back down, Harry," Evan said, pointing at him with his drink. "We're just talking. Let me understand this properly. You want us to avoid reporting the news because of a moral issue?"

"It's to protect the people of Aberfan."

"You've spoken to them?"

"I'm not the only one who feels like this."

"First I've heard of it."

"You've heard of it now."

"Let it go. Look at George; he's come up trumps with a great scoop."

Harry raised his eyebrows. Evan looked at his watch. It was just after six in the evening. He picked up the phone, instructing Harry to stay where he was, and asked the newsdesk to send Julian in if he was back. A couple of minutes later, Julian stuck his head around Evan's door.

"How's the Doxsey story going?" Evan said to him.

"Really interesting. Do you know what came out in court?

It's a bit weird. Harry, you remember Doxsey told us that Scotland Yard hadn't spoken to him when we saw him?"

"Yes," Harry said, although he struggled to recall and wasn't even sure if he'd been there when the exchange took place.

"They spoke to him on the weekend before. It's unbelievable."

Evan nodded at both of them. "It's a shame the pair of you can't get on with the rest of Thomson House in the same way."

Harry returned to find the day's *Telegraph*, 6 October, sitting on his desk with a note from Huw asking whether he had seen the magazine. Harry unfolded the paper and lifted it out. The front featured an illustration based on the nursery rhyme 'Three Blind Mice'. Charles Addams, who was behind *The Addams Family*, had recently brought out a children's book and the magazine featured a number of his typically ghoulish illustrations.

Harry flicked through the pages looking for whatever Huw meant for him to read. He was momentarily confused by a painting of Clyngwyn Falls in Brecon, but it was only an advert for Shell maps and guides. When he turned the page, he knew why Huw had left it with him. There was a six-page story by their reporter, John Summers, on Aberfan's fight for the entire £1,800,000 Disaster Fund. Underneath the headline was a picture of two fathers. They carried a placard asking where the money was and claiming that it had been spent. The narrative underneath the photograph described them as 'militant Aberfan survivors'.

The feature was about a battle in Aberfan between the parents and Gerald Davies, a new barrister who had been appointed Treasurer of the Aberfan Disaster Fund Committee. Both sides were cast in the poorest light. It relied on interviews, mainly from the two fathers the Welsh Office had already expressed concern to Harry about. The pair were portrayed as physically threatening and potentially violent. While John

Summers of *The Daily Telegraph* was taking his notes in Aberfan, he had apparently witnessed one of the fathers threaten to knock out another journalist who had merely expressed concern about the villager's health. The fathers were quoted as happy to have the support of the 'dynamite squad' of the sometimes violent end of Welsh nationalism: the Free Wales Army. A threat by this nationalist group to blow up Merthyr Town Hall was included and at least one other parent was portrayed as volunteering to assist. Another man interviewed was described as 'a short little Aberfan bereaved father with the inflamed face of an infuriated jockey'. Only one or two sentences were devoted to the parents who wanted to promote forgiveness and rejected the help of the Free Wales Army.

Gerald Davies, on the other hand, was described as uneasy, cocooned in his brand new Merthyr office with its panoramic view. The implication was that Gerald Davies was using the money to look after himself and his own interests. The story was not subtle. There were also those in the village who believed the money had been stolen by Gerald Davies so he could spend it on Merthyr town. *The Telegraph* was pitting people in the village against each other and setting Aberfan against Merthyr.

Harry glared repeatedly at the *Western Mail* desk. He was trying to read the offending story through again but the impromptu party taking place kept on distracting him. The whole newsroom had heard about how George, visiting his sister in London, had found himself caught up in the anti-Vietnam War protests outside the American embassy. Harry, almost in shock at *The Daily Telegraph*'s take on the mood in the village where 'the reality of a battlefield of human emotions is revealed' and 'hysteria is always in the air', found the noise and camaraderie in the newsroom excruciating. Who the hell cares about George's rubbish, Harry thought, or Doxsey, come to that?

He made himself a coffee and tried to ignore the *Western*

Mail reporters. He watched them snatch up their jackets, presumably heading for the pub as they cracked jokes. He found it ridiculous that Evan and everyone else seemed to think George had done something great. They all knew the real story. George had taken one of the tele-ad girls with him to London. His poor sister must have had more than just his reckless journalistic behaviour to be annoyed about. The man's personal behaviour was equally reckless and selfish.

As George and his colleagues on the *Western Mail* passed his desk, Harry glared and muttered under his breath. A couple of younger journalists heard and stopped for a second before continuing their conversation and jogging to catch up with their team clattering down the stairs. Harry assumed their intention was to ignore him. When George returned, followed by a few of his more junior staff, he knew he'd assumed wrong.

"What's your problem?"

"Nothing."

"What's this about? If you've got something to say, then come out and say it."

"What's going on out here?" Evan asked, approaching.

He'd finally been on his way out when he noticed the confrontation. The editor led his chief journalist, morose and uncommunicative, back into his office.

"I don't have time for this nonsense. I hoped, given time, you might get back to your old self. I thought Julian might do you good – working with someone new."

"A pariah! Even the tea lady knows he's related to Taylor."

"Nonsense! And you enjoy working with him more than you're letting on."

Harry leaned back in his chair, dejected but with something calculating and defiant in his eyes. He had to play the game for the Welsh Office. Harry put his fingers on the rim of the glass he had used earlier and absently turned it in a clockwise direction. If he was going to pull it off the way they were suggesting, he'd have to show more cooperation. He'd been stupid. He had to get everyone onside, including George and Mr Taylor.

"I was out of order," Harry said. "I'll apologise."

Evan, as he added a little water to his bonsai with a tin milk jug pinched from the canteen, looked up, worried.

Chapter 22

As Harry passed the newsdesk the following morning, Huw grabbed him and explained Merthyr Council had called.

"They're upset by the initial screening of a BBC film on Aberfan. The Director of Education is furious, too. He hasn't seen it himself but a number of teachers were there and they've filled him in. Not happy at all. The broadcast is on the twelfth."

Huw laid his open *Daily Mail* down on a stack of national newspapers and smoothed the pages out as he went back to his reading. Either Huw or his colleagues on the desk went through the papers every day in case there was anything which might have a Welsh connection. They were often lucky. Even on Suez they'd managed to get a piece out of a Welsh mother whose son was over there.

Harry wasn't sure whether to go directly to the Town Clerk in Merthyr or speak to the Welsh Office first. There were a few other stories he had to work on and he decided to get them out of the way. There was another story Harry didn't want to cover, but he didn't see how he could bury it. The newsdesk wanted him to meet Councillor Terry Richards. Harry knew Terry vaguely. The last time they had met, he'd interviewed the councillor about juvenile problems. He was a hairy, stocky man with a keen sense of humour. Harry was told the councillor had joined the fight to clear the Taff of pollution. If it was another complaint feature, Harry wanted to ignore it. They'd had more than enough complaints published in Postbag. Harry had a suspicion that Richards had already read his absurdly optimistic story on the Taff.

"I'm up to my eyes," Harry said. "Can't someone else cover it?"

"I thought you handled everything relating to the Taff."

"I'll speak to Evan," he said.

Approaching his editor's office, Harry didn't think he was in. The light was off, but when Harry peeped around the door, Evan was slumped in his chair, a cup of black coffee going cold in front of him. His blinds were half drawn.

"Had a good night?" Harry said, snapping the light on.

"Turn that off!"

"That's a yes."

"Heavy night, but it was interesting. Professor Northcote Parkinson says Wales should have its own kind of a parliament, more for administrative common sense than nationalist demands. I asked him if he'd write a piece for the paper. He's working from the American management model."

"American?"

"He had a point about the British Empire. Whitehall was all well and good when they had to administer Canada, India, Australia and what they held of Africa, but the days of the Empire are over. The Americans, of course, are all about decentralisation. They don't discuss education in Congress. I think it'll make an interesting feature."

"Look, what do you want me to do about this bloody Taff story?"

"Stop bothering me and go and see Terry. There's no one else available."

Harry was to meet Terry at his home off Loudon Square, situated to the south, at about halfway between Thomson House and the Bristol Channel. Running late, he jumped on a bus. When he was seated he ran his hand in an arc across the condensation on the window and watched the rivulets run their crooked way to the plastic black sill. The bus had seen better days. As rain hammered on the vehicle's roof, Harry shifted uncomfortably and realised he was sitting on a three-inch tear in the brown seat. He recalled a story he had done a year and a half before about kids taking penknives to bus seats and the fact that loneliness and frustration might have a lot to do with it. The fellow next to him had a heavy cold and sniffed wetly every few seconds. This grated on Harry to the point that, by the time he got off the bus, he believed that if he'd had a penknife to hand he might well have plunged the blade into the seat himself. Harry, hurrying to Terry's residence, resolved that the time had come to stop walking or getting buses and start relying on the Vauxhall again.

Terry's was a modern and modest house, but the boxy front garden had been taken over by an unruly fir tree. It reminded Harry of a large bear trapped in a small cage. Like the furry arms of such a bear, the branches of the tree had wrapped around the ornamental iron grille set into the top of the front wall. Terry was at the door immediately, and he promptly led his guest through to the dim lounge. They sat down, flanked by two lively Collie crosses with bad breath. Doggy portraits of the pair adorned a large Ercol sideboard. Harry listened as Terry explained he wanted South Wales anglers to write in with their ideas on cleaning up the Taff. His aim was to present the suggestions in a report to the city's councillors and the Glamorgan River Authority. Harry tidied up a neat quote from Terry about the river being a potentially beautiful resource. He wondered how on earth he could spin the story in a way that wouldn't displease the Welsh Office, until Terry provided him with the answer: his personal dream for the Taff. Terry wanted Cardiff to implement sections of the Buchanan plan, which would mean walling the banks of the Taff. Riverside paths would add to its charm and if a lock and weir were installed at Clarence Bridge, the city could hire out boats. Harry brightened at the thought of birds and boats. It sounded idyllic. That was exactly how Harry would write it.

"Do you fish?" Harry asked.

"I'm an angler," Terry said, "but I don't fish in the Taff any longer. What about you?"

"No."

"Happy to show you the ropes."

"Sure. Love to," Harry said, unable to think of anything worse than standing in the rain with a fishing rod.

By the time Harry returned to the office, he was soaked through. His umbrella had finally given out. The prolonged heavy rain had, more worryingly, resulted in an increase in calls. Harry listened to Huw's list of incidents reported to the newsdesk. People were panicking about further tip slides as slurry dams burst. There was no way he could avoid writing about those stories, especially when two little boys, aged two and four, had been snatched up by their mother as a flood of slurry raced towards them down a railway line. Harry took Huw's information and spent a good hour putting the stories together. He was halfway through when he became aware of Evan behind him. He didn't interrupt Harry, but Harry sensed his editor was reading over his shoulder as he typed. Harry was surprised that Evan would do such a thing. He'd worked for editors in Fleet Street who behaved like this, but he'd always appreciated Evan's sensitivity to stressful behaviour. And yet here he was putting the pressure on. Harry felt a self-conscious heat spreading across his back. He was also aware of a growing tension in his arms and fingers. Hyperaware, he calmed himself by recalling how he'd managed to get stories out with worse editors looking over his shoulder. He leaned forward towards his keyboard, putting a fraction more distance between them and blocking out some of Evan's view. Harry consciously relaxed his shoulders. He typed on, albeit a fraction more aggressively than normal, and managed to hide any trace of discomfort from his editor.

"This is good, Harry. Worrying times," Evan said.

"Two tip slides in Monmouthshire. In Pontypool, people had to be rescued from their homes."

"Aberfan. That's what everyone will be thinking. But I can't see that you've mentioned it."

"It's lazy journalism to keep referencing the disaster."

"Are you saying I'm lazy?"

"No, I'm saying we should make this a broader call that the NCB remove the tips immediately."

"This will shock you, Harry, but it's relevant to this story and it sells. The reason people are worried is because of Aberfan."

"We don't have to insult our readers' intelligence. We don't have to shoehorn it into every story."

"You want to watch it, Harry. You'll go too far one of these days. You include Aberfan. And I thought you'd want to know George is writing a complaint about the Welsh Office."

"And you're sharing this because...?"

"You seem to be in with them over there."

"In with them?"

"Huw saw you coming out of there the other day with Idris. Said you were thick as thieves. And then Ifor Davies was at the Business Club last night. Said you were a good man to have around."

Harry tried to look surprised but knew he had failed.

"Bollocks. I hardly know either of them. It's choir. That's probably it. What's the complaint about?"

"You'll have to ask George. *Western Mail* stuff."

Harry gave a sigh of relief as Evan left. He was astonished at the physical reaction someone reading over his shoulder produced; his temperature had gone up. Harry thought of Julian and how the boy had a lot to learn. That was a skill, to keep your cool with someone watching and reading.

Once Harry had finished typing, he gave the stories to the subs and chatted to one of them while the other read through. The working sub added the headline: 'Two Babies Pulled from Path of Raging Slurry' and changed 'boys' to 'babies' in Harry's introduction. Harry objected, telling the sub that it was stretching the truth too far because 'babies' implied gurgling infants.

"Exactly," said the sub. "Everyone loves stories about babies."

"I don't love stories about babies," Harry said.

"Everybody does," insisted the sub.

Such sensationalism made Harry feel entirely justified in having, contrary to his editor's instructions, left out any mention of the Aberfan disaster.

After Evan's comment about his closeness to the Welsh Office, Harry wasn't sure whether to speak to George, but there was a chance it might heal the rift between them, and he might, while he was at it, glean some information. Decided, he approached George's desk and loitered.

"Hello, George," he said, looking at the illegible notes on the desk, which wasn't much tidier than Harry's own.

"Harry."

"Just speaking to Evan," Harry said. "He told me you're writing about the Welsh Office. Some sort of complaint."

"And your interest is...?"

"I know Idris and George Thomas. Not well, but they're in my choir. I've got their numbers..."

"Already written, thanks. Not much to it, really. Alderman Elwyn Hughes – have you heard of him?"

"Yes," Harry lied.

"Rhondda Borough Council. The Welsh Office were sent some letters from Ferndale and Maerdy about the bus fares going up. The Welsh Office were particularly unhelpful. That's it, pretty much."

"Oh, well. If you need me for anything, just say."

"Thanks," George said, typing without looking up.

Harry turned to head back to his desk. What a stupid non-story, he thought. How typical of George. It was the kind of story George would berate other writers for doing. What an obnoxious hypocrite the man was.

"One minute, Harry."

"Yes?"

"We had a meeting about Aberfan yesterday."

"So?"

"We're serialising Tony Austin's book on the disaster – right up until the memorial service."

"That's a good idea," said Harry.

"Thanks," George replied. "My idea. The book's out on the anniversary. If you want to buy a copy, it's thirty shillings."

What a coup this was for Harry. It was just what the Welsh Office had asked for. Harry considered that he might have been playing his own abilities down. It just went to show that nobody really knew what they might be capable of until they tried. While Harry was aware that he hadn't been entirely fair in the way he went about it, it was very easy to convince himself that George would have done exactly the same thing to him if given the chance.

Harry wanted to gloat over his achievement with Idris, the only person who would understand. The serialisation would perfectly justify Idris' faith in him. Harry called and asked if he was free. They agreed to meet in the Poacher's Lodge immediately. The old journalist gathered up his things and exited the building.

The rain had eased and left a grey sky, but more of it wasn't far away. Leaves had been churned underfoot until the pavements were coated with a wet mulch resembling conker-coloured bran. Roads glistened, painfully bright. Harry headed straight over the bridge and turned into Sophia Gardens, walking alongside the Taff. A sudden burst of sun bathed the wet, leafy banks in citron light. The Taff, rolling along, blackly reflected them. A woodpigeon, perhaps celebrating the temporary break from being rained on, hoot-hoot-hooted with the determined monotony of a child practising the same note on a recorder. Harry couldn't imagine fishing in the river, let alone eating fish from it, but he felt a sudden surge of happiness. The raindrops glittered. This is Wales, he thought; the black, rain-soaked soil and the sun-dappled leaves; there was something romantic about it. You didn't have to go far out of the city to be among the old stone chapels, shimmering fields and the shelter of ancient trees like oak and cedar, whitebeam and yew.

Harry liked the Poacher's Lodge as it reminded him of a mushroom thanks to its disproportionate red-tiled roof and ground floor of grey stone. He had to walk around a vast puddle to reach the door. Inside, Idris was already waiting for him. They sat near the bar. Harry looked at the lofty shelves between the bar top and ceiling. The rows of dusty, labelled bottles reminded him of a library.

"First things first," Idris said, "these pieces about the beauty of Wales. I'm pleased to a point. Lovely feature on Aberdare. Lovely feature on Brecon the other week. But this week?"

"Caerphilly?

"Yes. Not that I'm telling you how to do your job, but you've got a picture of the Right Honourable Ness Edwards saying Caerphilly is a good place to live."

"Yes?"

Idris dropped the paper on the table and tapped the picture of the Caerphilly Labour MP. Harry knew Ness Edwards as someone who disliked Plaid as much as George Thomas did.

"He looks like he's just discovered Caerphilly is built on toxic waste ground."

"I don't take the pictures, Idris."

"If you can't get a nice photograph of a Welsh person or place, then please, for God's sake, use an artist's impression."

Harry stared at Idris, surprised and put out by the authoritative tone his acquaintance had adopted. He was at the point of saying something in riposte to remind Idris he wasn't an employee of the Welsh Office, but then he realised that Idris may well have been joking. He decided to give him the benefit of the doubt.

"How's it going, anyway?" Idris continued.

"George isn't going to be writing much on Aberfan. Tony

Austin's book is being serialised instead."

"Champion."

"This BBC thing? Any update?"

"That's why I wanted to speak to you. They had the advance screening and all hell's broken loose. They mentioned four Merthyr councillors who hadn't visited this injured lad. Not true. Not true at all. All the councillors have been to see him. Well, three had, and the fourth wrote to the boy."

"And they can prove they attended?" Harry asked.

"Yes. It's all documented. And apparently there's a lot of criticism about the rehousing of victims. What could we do? Most didn't want to leave Aberfan. I can understand why they're not happy at the way the BBC are spinning it."

"The newsdesk said something about the Director of Education."

"I don't know much about that, I'm afraid. I'd have to watch the film."

"And the film is going out next week?"

"Yes. Selwyn Jones, Merthyr's Town Clerk, has written to the producer of the documentary, Ivor Dunkerton at the BBC. He's also written a complaint to *The Daily Telegraph* about the erroneous distortion of what is actually happening in the village."

"The supplement?"

"Yes," Idris said.

"It's disgusting. Have you ever read anything as ridiculous as the idea that Gerald Davies has already spent the entire fund on Merthyr? Why don't they understand that such a large sum has to be invested? As if Gerald Davies should simply stuff almost two million in cash into one of the mattresses in Aberfan – to later divide up over the kitchen table before handing it out to the parents. It's nothing more than a financial misunderstanding which is being manipulated by *The Telegraph* – if not created by the press in the first place!"

"It's terrible."

"You don't have to worry about it," Harry said. "I'm handling it already. I agree with you. They've gone too far."

"But you're not going to tell me what you can do?

"Not yet."

"Well, here's a copy of Selwyn's complaints: one to *The Telegraph* and one to the BBC."

Idris handed Harry the two copies. Harry read *The Daily Telegraph* letter first. While he believed that *The Telegraph* was completely in the wrong, he felt that a complaint letter was the wrong way to get the newspaper's attention. You had to fight fire with fire. As Harry read the correspondence, he realised it would only serve to make matters worse. He could just imagine what *The Telegraph* editor might make of it. If anything, it served to rather piously remind the paper what their job was. Reading the journalist's unhappy expression, Idris defended himself:

"A London barrister advised that we should prepare a statement of objections and send them to the editor. He thought *The Telegraph* would then find a way to publish an article of a different tone in a couple of months."

Fat chance, thought Harry. He read the penultimate paragraph again:

Journalism is a time-honoured profession of great responsibility, and those who pursue it have their reputations to uphold and maintain. Everyone knows that newspapers are carefully read by millions of people. There is a duty incumbent on those responsible for producing them to ensure that articles are written by men and women who know their subject thoroughly and who can report accurately. Your article is in the worst possible taste and must be an example of the worst type of reporting. My council have felt and still feel that the best interests of the residents of Aberfan would be served if the people were allowed to lead a normal village life without any outside interference by Television or Press Authorities.

Fortunately, Selwyn's second letter, to the BBC, raised specific problems and inaccuracies in the film which *The Telegraph* letter, to its detriment, had not. This would allow Harry to bury the story for a bit. The film wasn't being broadcast for another week and, presumably, they would be editing in light of the feedback they had received. He could legitimately tell the newsdesk that the story was still running and he'd have to wait and see what the final film was like.

"So how is the Lay Off Aberfan campaign being thought of at the *Echo*?"

"I'm working on it," Harry said.

"We're counting on you now, you know."

Harry walked Idris back to Park Place. After he had gone, Harry felt weary. He wondered if Julian was still at the Law Courts. He looked at his watch and realised that Julian would probably have left half an hour before. Harry strolled back to Thomson House, musing on what he had left to write up. It would be a late one. He was glad to see Julian hunched and frowning over his typewriter, stabbing at the keys as fast as he could.

"Going well?" Harry asked.

"Very well. Even without planning permission for a petrol filling station, a profit would have been made. Doxsey had an offer of close to fifty thousand pounds from a supermarket. His defence is going to have to work hard."

"Silly man."

"And he's sticking it to your Labour friends. He said Iorwerth Jones is against – hang on, I've got it written down: 'He is against petrol filling stations anywhere, not only on corners'. I thought that was a good quote."

"Keeping the thing balanced. Well done."

"Are you sure I'm not writing too much? I mean, I filled half the paper yesterday."

"We can't all be in court. Think of it like that. You are our eyes and ears. Anything we know comes from you. The more detail, the better for the *Echo*. Give it colour. Let us know everything."

"Thanks a lot, Harry," Julian said. "I mean it."

"I'd better let you get on."

"I'm going to be here all night as it is. Five minutes won't make a difference."

As Harry sat back at his typewriter, it occurred to him that if it all went wrong, a 'Lay Off Harry' campaign might have its attractions.

Chapter 23

"Right," Evan said. "How are you finding Harry?"

"Fine," Julian replied with the brightest of smiles.

"Ask me how I'm doing."

"How are you doing?"

"I have an ominous feeling."

"I'm sorry to hear that."

"Let me tell you a story. When I was a reporter, there was another fellow I worked with. He'd done a lot of good investigative work. The only thing was, he became obsessed with Freemasons. He saw them and their dealings everywhere. Maybe in some cases he was right. The problem was, he had no evidence. Before long, he was working straight off crackpot conspiracy theories."

"What happened to him?"

"The editor sacked him, of course."

"Why are you telling me? I've never written anything about Freemasons."

"Swap my former colleague for Harry and Freemasons for a lay off campaign."

"What's a 'lay off campaign'? I don't get it."

"I don't know how much he's told you, but I'm going to have to pull him back into line."

As if subliminally thinking of the pulling in store, Evan tugged at his tie from knot to end and aligned it over the buttons on his creased shirt. He looked thoughtfully at Julian. Evan crossed his legs and leaned back in his chair.

"Do you have any idea how far this has gone?" Evan noted the rapidity with which the boy's smile faded. "You're writing a lot. And Harry doesn't seem to be writing too much these days. He used to write reams of the stuff. Now it's you and this

Doxsey case."

"You still haven't explained about the campaign?"

Evan didn't respond.

"Is there something wrong with the writing?" Julian asked.

"No, but you're writing half the paper. Harry's up to something and I want to know what."

Julian looked doubtful and said nothing.

"Is Harry investigating something I don't know about?" Evan asked.

"Like what?"

"Huw tells me the Welsh Office has called and asked for Harry a number of times. What the hell is going on?"

"I don't think there's anything going on. He's been off-diary this week so he's been giving me a hand. Perhaps that's why he hasn't had much time to write. I don't know what the Welsh Office's involvement is. You know Harry – he's a man with a lot of friends. Perhaps he's got something planned for the memorial service. That's probably it. Or maybe he's got an investigation going on into the Welsh Office."

"An investigation, huh?"

"He's investigating something. That's something I do know."

The boy was loyal. Evan ground his cigarette out and decided it was time to end the conversation. He wasn't going to get anywhere. He could see that.

"I think he's working on something personal," Julian said. "This trial finishes tomorrow, anyway."

"Fine. But if it comes to the anniversary and we've got nothing but your copy, there's going to be trouble for both of you. He can't launch a one-man campaign."

When Harry returned to the newsroom he found Julian sitting crossed-legged on their desk with a cigarette dangling from his fingers. Jumping down as soon as he spotted the expression on Harry's face, the boy joined him at the newsdesk. Evan joined them as well, leaning his back against the edge of it. Harry looked curiously at Evan to his right and Julian to his left, although none of them said a word.

"What's the news on the BBC film?" Huw asked.

"It's a non-story," Harry said.

Julian and Evan looked at each other. Evan arched his eyebrows.

"How come?" Huw said.

"Everything remotely controversial was edited out. By the sounds of it, Dunkerton got scared, so he's tightened up. Very cautious. Edited out anything originally based on conflicts of evidence or inconsistent accounts by witnesses."

"So there's no story?"

"Does it sound like there's a story?"

"Fine. I'll scratch it."

Huw grabbed a pen and drew a line through the third item on his list. The spiking of another story related to Aberfan was hard for Julian to watch, especially with Evan overseeing the whole process. Evan stared at Julian to the point that the boy began to fidget nervously. Julian rubbed the back of his neck and returned to his work. Harry and Huw continued chatting about yesterday's news as Evan looked on.

"I need to talk to you later," Evan said to Harry, breaking into the conversation by placing a hand on his shoulder. "I'm going out, but I'll be back and you better be here."

"What's up?" Harry jogged after him. "Look Evan, I need to talk to you."

"When I get back."

"I'll walk with you."

"This had better not be what I think it is."

Evan's tone had been dismissive and he was in a hurry, but he remained in front of Harry.

"Maybe I haven't explained it properly," Harry said.

"How long have you been in this business? The Nationals have already decided what they're going to run. You can't really think that when they have their journalists out working on whatever stories they've got, they'll read Harry's Lay Off Aberfan campaign and say: 'Christ. We better lay off. Stop the press. Harry from the *South Wales Echo* has a point. Pulp it all, boys!'"

"That's very funny."

"What you should do, if you want to do something for that poor bloody village, is write the best stories you can."

"Hmm."

"Two days ago, Julian wrote so much we could have dedicated the whole bloody paper to Doxsey's case. The subs spoke to him and he said that you told him to write as much as he could."

"I just meant that he should prove himself."

"You're filling the paper. If this has anything to do with the Lay Off Aberfan campaign—"

"I've written plenty of things recently on Aberfan."

"You're up to something. Is this to do with Doxsey?"

"Doxsey? It's nothing to do with Doxsey. Doxsey's over."

"The Welsh Office, then? Have you found something out? Are you investigating something?"

The two men stared at each other.

"Yes," Harry said. "Something big."

Chapter 24

The Secretary of State leant out of the limousine to welcome Harry in. After a while people ceased to notice Cledwyn Hughes' port-wine birthmark, but he still looked oddly dishevelled with his small, sad eyes blinking behind large square-framed glasses. Cledwyn was visibly exhausted. Harry wasn't surprised. The Secretary of State for Wales, as Head of the Welsh Office, had to represent Wales at home and abroad, as well as ensure that Wales was never overlooked by the UK government. Idris, on the other hand, looked much brighter, and when he and Harry shook hands, Harry found his fears about visiting Aberfan abating a little. The Secretary of State explained the pristine car had once belonged to Harold Macmillan when he was Prime Minister. A waft of sweet pine from a discreet air freshener and the BBC presenters' quiet discussion on the radio served to relax Harry further. They were visiting to check on the progress of the memorial, which unfortunately wouldn't be finished in time for the memorial service. As the limousine sped towards Aberfan, Harry was told a slight delay in completion was the price you had to pay for something utterly unique and lasting.

The sky was endless, the blinding grey-white of a standard opaque lightbulb. Harry listened to the details of Cledwyn's recent trip to Scranton, Pennsylvania, and gazed at the tips on Merthyr's side – greyish purple, speckled with yellow vegetation.

Attracting stares, the chauffeur dropped them on Aberfan Road and was given instructions to pick them up later. Harry felt they all looked their age in the cold, pearl grey light. They planned to visit a few places and stop in the café on the way back. First they went to the school site. Three men in suits were having a meeting near the cleared area, where little remained other than the stone wall on the left side of the school. Harry didn't recognise any of them. He wondered if they were from Merthyr Council. By the time his group had finished their tour, the other party were disappearing into their cars. He assumed the villagers must be well used to parties of old men and their meetings.

They walked to the hillside cemetery and sat on a weather-beaten bench. Idris explained in detail the work being undertaken on the memorial and talked Harry through the design, including the plateau and the use of motif. Cledwyn talked more generally of Merthyr. They needed to make a concerted effort to bring back employers. He talked with passion, but like so many politicians, he had a rehearsed phraseology that Harry found grating. The old journalist switched off and let his hands do the notetaking. Sometimes he would read his shorthand back and barely remember hearing the words.

"Present employment," Cledwyn said with authority, "has been affected by the credit squeeze measures of June '66. Unemployment has rarely been less than 3.5 percent, but since July last year it's climbed to present high levels of 5.6 percent and occasionally higher. Merthyr Corporation have made strenuous efforts..."

Cledwyn continued to talk but Harry was distracted by the crows swooping over the firs. Turning, they sailed up until it hurt his eyes to follow them against the white sky, almost reverberating with brightness. Behind them the tarpaulin which screened the memorial work smacked softly in the wind. Harry realised Cledwyn was still talking:

"We're giving inducements to companies who sign up to commerce on the industrial estate."

"Such as?" Harry asked.

"Oh, building grants, plant investment grants, loans at moderate rates of interest and towards the total cost of working capital. What we really need is to get the word out. And it's people like you who can help us do it."

The three looked at the valley from their vantage point. The boughs of the fir trees which marked the cemetery boundary waved up and down in the wind as though imitating the beating wings of the crows that sailed around them. A pigeon shot across the sky. Autumn leaves tumbled in the wind. There was so much life and movement in the view. The crows tracked towards them and wheeled and circled high overhead, their rattling calls like chains on children's bikes in need of oiling. Only God should move mountains, Harry thought. Cledwyn put a hand on his shoulder.

"Harry? We've arranged with the Rector of St David's to reserve pews for members of the Welsh Office and our wives. You're welcome to sit with us. We're also sending a wreath. The memorial service starts at quarter past nine in the morning, so we'll meet you at nine. Feel free to bring your wife. Bridget, isn't it?"

What hadn't escaped Harry's notice was that Idris had given Cledwyn a conspiratorial wink when they thought Harry wasn't looking.

They were getting cold and headed for Moy Road, which since the disaster started at number eleven. Cledwyn detailed the distance the spill had travelled, pointing to some indistinct houses further down, although Idris and Harry were only too aware. They headed for the café. An advert for tea, coffee, sandwiches and hotdogs was painted in white capital letters on the flyblown windowpanes.

The café was packed with local customers. At the back there was a glass display counter with wilting sandwiches, fruit buns and jam doughnuts, a dry chocolate Swiss roll and two rows of Kit Kats. A cylinder of paper-wrapped drinking straws stood on top. Underneath, an A4 sign read, 'no credit'. The Formica tables each had their own salt and pepper pots and sugar cubes, along with bottles of tomato ketchup wearing collars of drying, air-exposed red sauce. A girl with bleached hair and dirty white pumps had to return twice to remind herself what they had ordered. Harry wasn't impressed, but Idris introduced Harry and Cledwyn to her when she brought over their drinks.

A young woman nursing a baby and having a Coke with her friend volunteered to talk to them after overhearing.

"My family are from Aberfan, but my husband and I were in Liverpool at the time. He needed work, you see. When I saw it on the news, I phoned my husband and told him we needed to go straight home. We caught the first train. He'd lost his cousin and her family. They were the last to be found. Everyone was at the school, you see. It was a priority to get the children out of the school. The houses had to wait until later."

The young woman talked and Harry unwound as he listened.

"And you remained here?" he asked.

"Yes. My husband went back to Liverpool, though only to work out his notice."

Even Idris was aware of Harry's palpable relief, though he had no idea of its source. Harry and the woman talked candidly until Harry had filled a couple of pages in his notebook.

"Is there anyone else we could speak to?" he asked her.

"Yes. My neighbour might talk to you."

And in that short moment, the woman from Aberfan had made Harry understand that nobody had been obsessed with his personal behaviour in Aberfan, save for him.

When Harry returned to the newsroom, he was aware of a subtle shift in mood. A couple of the subs were notably tense. Unable to work out whether it was the *Western Mail* team, the *Echo* team or something to do with his efforts being discovered, he sat tight. Julian, who had already tipped him off that Evan was watching, was busy writing a story about a child having got lost on a mountain.

It was just as Harry was slumped in his chair, arms linked

over his stomach and his chin on his chest, that his musings were violently interrupted.

Evan had been visited by a councillor friend of his and the pair had hit the Jack Daniels after the councillor took a trip to the Co-op. Roaring drunk and well into reminiscing about the war, a game of 'who could kill who quicker' had developed into threatening one-upmanship. The councillor had playfully grabbed the Echo editor in a headlock and Evan failed to see the funny side. Frustrated at the drunken assault by his friend, Evan resolved to teach the guy a lesson. By the time they had burst out of Evan's office and fallen to the floor in the reporters' room, they were actively trying to kill each other.

"I could kill you with one chop," Evan said, red-faced.

"And I could kill you with one finger," the councillor screamed back.

It was Julian who came to the rescue. Still unused to such dramatics in the workplace, he was shocked while the rest of the newsroom sat and watched with wry amusement. Julian knelt down beside the wrestling pair and reminded Evan that the councillor wasn't worth going to prison for. It wasn't so much Julian's voice of reason that stopped the fight, more the awareness that people were starting to laugh. Julian and Huw helped the pair up and insisted the councillor leave and Evan sleep it off in his office.

The following morning, the mood in the newsroom hadn't changed. Evan was hungover and defensive in light of the previous day's incident. A whisper went through the building that Evan was best left alone. It wasn't just the Echo staff who were behaving strangely, and Harry knew something was going on. There was a sense of waiting in the newsroom. It didn't seem to be anything good. When Evan came out of his office and motioned for Harry to follow him inside, there seemed to be a perceptible buzz of anticipation.

"I've heard something interesting," Evan said, sitting down.

"Oh?" Harry said, nervously clearing his throat.

Evan looked grey.

"George and Steve were out last night."

"Right."

"They met some of the junior staff of the Welsh Office."

Harry scratched his head.

"And?"

"The Welsh Office were talking about a journalist."

"Right."

"Rumour has it, this journalist will print whatever they tell him." Evan folded his arms and stared at Harry, whose focus was lost in the middle distance. "That would be enough, but I heard something a few weeks ago that I could hardly believe until now. You had a report given to you anonymously?"

"What report?"

"Civil Defence? The lessons everyone can learn after Aberfan?"

"It's been completely discredited."

"By the Welsh Office?"

"Yes."

"They commissioned it," Evan shouted. "That's a story in itself!"

Harry went to speak but checked himself, not sure of what to say.

"I've got to let you go, Harry. Nobody wants you here. You can't be trusted. You get given good stories that you then avoid writing about. Events happen and you're making your own decisions as to whether they're newsworthy or not. You don't get paid to sit around and agonise over ethics. I need writers who write. I know exactly what you've been up to on Aberfan."

Harry heard the words, but only as an echoing distortion, as if Evan were speaking at one end of a tunnel and he was at the other. Knowing that Harry would need to process what he had said, Evan gave him a minute to let the words sink in. The old journalist sat there feeling queasy but experiencing a strange sense of déjà vu. He had imagined this happening as the worst-case scenario. Evan lost patience and realised he'd prefer it if the old man argued back rather than stand there looking lost.

"You hear me, Harry? You've left me no choice."

Harry continued to stare back, mute and unprovoked. Evan realised he wasn't going to get what he wanted, which was for his journalist to show some passion for his job and, even better, to provide some forgivable explanation. Evan gave up and changed tack.

"I'm sorry that it's come to this. Look, old chap, get your things together. I'll get Julian to help you. Leave quietly down the backstairs. Don't worry; I'll put it in the nicest possible way."

While Evan had been talking, Harry had felt as though he was floating above himself and looking down. How strange it was, seeing things from such a different perspective, strange and then relaxing. He could breathe deeply again instead of the shallow, slightly winded gasps of a moment ago. It seemed as though an outside force had swept away any emotion. It didn't matter how or why this change had come about. What mattered was that his head was startlingly clear. The image of a chessboard came to mind. He felt at once that he was thinking with clarity, though there was also a recklessness surging through him. Why hadn't he felt like this at Aberfan? It was as if, with the final pressure of the situation, his mind was sorting the letters into sentences. Everything was rattling into place like the *Echo* and *Western Mail* machinists shot metal letters into the forme. Harry took a big breath in.

"Three weeks ago," Harry began, and listened to his own voice for any tremble of uncertainty. There wasn't one; his words were imbued with confidence. He sat up straighter and continued: "somebody called the newsdesk talking about the whole village being divided. They claimed those with surviving children believed the rest of the village was jealous. Then the

Press Association called and said the same thing. I made a couple of calls and it was bullshit."

With the last word, Harry brought his flat palm down on the desk. Evan sat back an inch, but a strange, fleeting look of genuine interest crossed his face. He nodded slightly to encourage Harry to continue.

"Oh, but the Nationals ran with it all right. Did they check anything? Did they hell! I checked, Evan. And it took me all day to get hold of Chris Sullivan from the Aberfan Parents' and Residents' Association, but thank God I did. He said this is happening so often with unscrupulous freelancers, he's now issuing bulletins to the community. Listen to me, Evan. Someone is playing amateur dramatics."

Evan pursed his lips. "PA are usually reliable."

"How do we know they're reliable if we don't check ourselves? After that, I started investigating the matter. I'm going to write a piece on it."

"So that's what you've been doing?"

"In part. It's going to centre on *The Telegraph*'s magazine story from the sixth of October."

"Oh Christ."

"You read it?"

"I didn't read it. I heard about it. Do you have a copy still?"

"Yes."

"Bring it in, then."

Harry went and fetched the magazine. On the way to his desk, he still felt the control he had mastered in Evan's office.

"There are a very small number of parents lashing out," Harry continued after returning and handing Evan the magazine, "which is hardly surprising after the way the NCB have behaved. But it's sheer distortion! Let's say, conservatively, four hundred mothers and fathers had children killed, injured or directly involved in the Aberfan disaster. A handful are supplying stories. Fleet Street just aren't checking their facts and neither is PA. I'm putting together an exposé on it."

"Harry—"

"I'll bring you the exposé once it's done."

"If you want this crusade, you'll have to pursue it alone. We're not going to publish anything. You know we're not, but keep in touch."

"I never took you for naïve, Evan. When you know the whole truth, you'll be every bit as outraged as I am."

There was nothing for it but to call Idris and explain there would be no Lay Off Aberfan campaign. What a waste of time and effort on something which could have been brilliant. Harry thought back to all those meetings and his trip to Fleet Street. Well, that wasn't entirely wasted, Harry thought. He had caught up with Tom and the situation had naturally blocked off roads of progress until only one course remained. With the telephone handset held halfway between his desk and his ear, Harry reminded himself that Idris had never wanted the Echo to run the campaign. The civil servant had always thought it would be entirely overlooked where the Nationals were concerned. At least Harry had a plan B to fall back on. He'd have to go it alone from now on. He dialled the number, spoke to Idris' secretary and got through.

"Ah, Idris, I need to discuss a bit of a problem."

"What's wrong?"

"Forget the Lay Off Aberfan campaign. Evan's going mad. Some of your boys have been shouting their mouths off. They've let me go."

"What?"

"They've let me go."

"I don't understand."

"As we both know..."

"Are you all right?"

"Yes, fine. As we both know, an *Echo* campaign was never the original goal. You wanted the *Mirror*, Idris."

Harry was happy that he could at least throw that back at the civil servant. Idris could hardly have a go at Harry when his original idea was to get the support of the same national newspaper which supported Robens. He'll understand in the end, Harry thought.

"Get in there and persuade your editor to change his mind!"

The civil servant sounded noticeably upset, but Harry couldn't work out whether it was because their efforts had amounted to nothing or if Idris regretted their actions. Harry almost blurted out that things would be okay, almost told Idris they didn't even need the campaign. Instinct counselled him to hold back.

"It's over," Harry said, restricting himself from adding anything else.

"You promised us the campaign, Harry. We can still do it. You can work for us, for God's sake. Do you want to churn out your little local stories or do you want to change the country?"

"I'll see you at choir," Harry said.

Harry collected his belongings, feeling both sick and curiously elated. He was relieved that Julian had disappeared so that he didn't have to say goodbye. He shook hands with a few subs he had never really cared for. I'll be back soon enough, he told himself.

Outside, he turned to face the building with pride. He had spoken his mind. Everything he wanted to say had come to him and rolled off his tongue the way the papers roll off the press. He had surprised himself with the authority he employed when speaking to Evan and remembered the look of surprise on the editor's face. Their positions had changed for a fleeting moment. He had taken charge. He was inordinately proud of himself. He hadn't gone to pieces or slunk out. He'd put forward his side of things and if Evan wanted to let him go then that was Evan's prerogative. Harry had his plan. This unpleasant episode was merely just that. It was a small part of the overall game. He appeared to have lost, but this was exactly what he had intended to happen. He was in complete control.

Nevertheless, Harry sensed his euphoric feeling might wear

off. Without thinking too deeply, he endeavoured to draw out his feeling of elated triumph as long as he could. He put on the radio when he arrived home and sang along, stepping around the room in time to the music. I did the right thing for Wales, he thought, and they've all sought to punish me for it, but I am in the right.

It was hours later, in the middle of the night, that he awoke with horror. Harry sat straight up in bed, frozen. The curtains, undrawn, allowed the October moon to carpet the floor with four large, milky-hued diamonds. The moon shone down on him, cold and white, and its light glowed in his bedtime glass of water. How lonely and small he felt as Wales slept. A cold feeling of loss wrapped itself around him and Harry wondered about the elation that had filled him earlier in the evening. He felt as vulnerable as a child waking after a nightmare to find his parents gone. He leaned forward to where his clothes had been left at the end of what was Bridget's side of the bed. He tugged his knitted tank top over his check pyjama shirt. Seeking comfort more than warmth, Harry pulled the candy-striped wool blankets and candlewick up to his chin, then turned his face into the pillows. With dawn only an hour away, he tried not to submit to the feeling of being overwhelmed. Just before he slipped into confused dreams, Harry mistook the sound of the milk float in the street for the sound of the rotary presses in the great hall starting up and speeding through the gears.

Chapter 25

Harry would put the right questions to the right people when he reached the memorial service. He was so lost in thought about his story that he barely noticed the landscape whizzing by on the journey. Tree trunks were black with earlier rain. For a minute or two the sun burst out and turned the clouds into a vast gold haze over the valley. Then all too soon the sun was obscured and the day, once again, reverted to being dismal and damp. Drizzle began to lick at the windows. Harry watched a drop at eye level split into a needle of silver beads under the force of the Vauxhall's speed and the wind.

Upon arriving, Harry, crossing the Taff, stopped to watch the swollen river race in the direction he had come from. There was something hypnotic about the fretful eddies and currents. As long as I stick to my plan, he thought, I'll be fine.

Harry attended the service in St David's but sat at the back of the packed church and left immediately afterwards to avoid the Welsh Office families, catching only a glimpse of them as they greeted each other before the mass began. He didn't want anyone threatening to interfere from this point on. Outside the church, he donned the trilby that had been placed on his knees throughout the service and pulled the brim down low.

The bereaved held close to each other, pinched and silent. Inevitably, the media was everywhere. There were crowds of journalists and broadcasters on the site of the school. Microphones. Cameras. These were the people he interviewed without them even being aware of it. He talked to them leisurely, enquiring about their stories. They were frank with him.

For a good half an hour he chatted with an American

photographer from *LIFE Magazine*. The photographer had spent five weeks in Aberfan at the time of the disaster, lodging at the Mackintosh Hotel. He had approached the tragedy with a good measure of sensitivity and he tried hard to win the locals around. Surprised at the way others of his profession had behaved, the photographer explained that he'd photographed a camera team doing a stand-up item in the ruins of a building demolished by slurry. Harry felt solidarity in that he too had turned the lens on his own profession.

Keeping a low profile, Harry made his notes and sought out fresh comment. He spotted George across the cemetery, the wind ruffling his curls, and shifted his position so that he was hidden by a stone plinth. More visitors drifted in. They were slower now, trudging up the hill to the cemetery. It was hardly a surprise that the village seemed so worn down. Flowers were everywhere – red roses and sprays of orange and yellow carnations.

Once he had enough material, Harry left the cemetery. What he'd heard was hard to take. He wanted to distance himself from these outside media people. He turned his collar up to the bitter east wind and made his way to the Taff again to inspect the state of the water, clear his thoughts and think about the structure of his piece.

He would write a small, secondary piece about Aberfan and its present position, the clear-up operation and the band of slime visible still. Attempts were being made to camouflage the scarred landscape. Meadow flowers had been planted for the spring. It would take a predicted six months to remove 250,000 tons of colliery rubbish. There was drainage work to be done. In another eighteen months or so, a new junior and infant school would be complete. A swimming pool was being built with sponsorship money: Mr Pastry's Pool.

Mist again capped the mountains and the smell of wood smoke hung in the air. Benwell Fireworks were on sale in W H Smith & Son. Toffee apples could be bought in the grocers and

Bonfire Night was on the way. In the cemetery, the lanterns would burn nightlong.

Harry walked back in the direction of the train station with the intention of strolling along the banks of the Taff. The Buchanan plan of walling the river, proposed by Councillor Terry Richards, sprang to mind. They were going to be high sides if Terry Richards had his way. Harry wondered how much faster the river would flow. You wouldn't want that on a day like this, he thought. It was probably a good thing that it twisted and turned and had to wend its foamy way over rocks and roots.

He stood uncertainly amidst the pleasantly organic-smelling vegetation, wondering about the best way to get to the edge of the river. A wave of sad calm came over him as he picked his way down, holding onto rotting branches and avoiding the brambles and spongy mounds of clogged leaves. The deep and fast river ran quiet enough that birds could be heard in all directions. An unseen one made kissing noises, chirrups and trilling whistles. Harry turned to the water, put his hand to his forehead and rubbed down over his eyes as though massaging a headache. It wasn't as though the rain would flush the river clean. More slurry would make its filthy way into the water and more coal dust would be washed down. He heard the sound of another train arriving and noted minutes later a trickle of people crossing the bridge.

Harry was entranced by the river. He could have stood by it for hours. He observed the fresh muddy erosion of the banks as the water rubbed and bumped and pummelled, blindly feeling for its track to the sea. He watched the submerged clumps of grass waving in the current like sea anemones. He stared at the trees lining the opposite bank; their rustling signalled that the rain had started again. He wondered at the reason he thought more clearly by water. He was so lost in thought that when he heard someone call him the hairs on the back of his neck stood up.

"Hey, you!"

For a second, Harry thought it was someone about to warn him that he was dangerously close to the river, but he then he realised he recognised the person. Paul Falstone. He stood at the top of the bank looking down on Harry, and with a freshly lit cigarette in one hand, fixed him with a blunt gaze.

"I thought you'd gone. I've been looking for you. I was about to give up and get the train out," Falstone said to him in a terse tone.

"Can I help you?" Harry asked, adopting the same clipped, unfriendly manner.

"I don't know. Do you have some kind of problem?"

"In what way?"

"I've just had two journalists come up and talk about some altercation you and I had last year."

"An altercation?"

Harry stared fixedly up at Falstone, his brows knitted in surprise but saying nothing.

"Yes."

"I don't know what people are saying," Harry said.

"Of course you do."

Harry knew the conversation was taking a quite childish turn, but he didn't have any idea how to rectify it. And who had told Falstone? Had George realised and said something? The exertion of getting down to the water's edge had left him feeling clammy. It had been impossible to note particular details on the day of the disaster and now Harry saw how his memory had played tricks on him. He remembered Falstone with light, shaggy brown hair, but the Falstone above him had dark brown hair. It occurred to Harry that the colour of Falstone's jacket the year before had altered Harry's perception of his other features. Harry noted that Falstone's face looked sharp. His chin was pointed and he had bad skin. Deep creases had formed in his cheeks where once, in childhood, he presumably had dimples. It was a tough face. It reminded Harry of a rugby player he knew. Perhaps he doesn't play rugby, Harry thought. Perhaps he's just like me, out in all winds and weathers.

Harry was pleased that Falstone had not made a move to come down, but at the same time he did not enjoy being looked down upon and felt trapped. He was backed by the swirling water and he was starting to get wet. The rain was getting heavier. He only had one answer: stick to the plan.

"I even offered to work with you so I don't know what your problem is," Falstone said.

"You needed my help, more like."

"I won bloody Journalist of the Year off the back of my piece about Aberfan, you idiot!"

"You won an award?"

"That's right. Nice do in London. Lots of booze. Thanks very much."

"Let me ask you this, then. Does this place look like a battlefield to you? Are the streets full of fighting parents? No. Edwards and Bridges are fighting because they're angry. That's natural, but they're the minority."

"I don't know what you're talking about."

"They're both ill over this, you know. Edwards can't walk without a stick."

"If you're talking about *The Telegraph*, I didn't write it. I've never written for *The Telegraph*."

"Who the hell cares? You're all the same. I'm working on a piece which is going to be very interesting to you – very interesting indeed! I'm going to name and shame journalists and newspapers who are using the bereaved villagers for their own agenda."

Falstone smiled, raised his chin and shook his head in amusement.

"Out of curiosity, have you spoken to Edwards and Bridges?" Falstone asked.

Harry didn't offer a reply but turned back to the water for a second, startled by a noise. It was nothing and he turned his attention back to Falstone.

"So, who is this piece going to be for?" the Fleet Street journalist asked.

"Everyone. Everyone will know you're looking to do a bit of fishing and you're looking for the blackest water to cast your rod," Harry said, clambering up the steep bank.

He was unable to successfully get up the same way he'd descended and his slipping feet churned the mud into a greasy mush. His hands were filthy and he decided to pick along the bank a little further where the climb might be easier. His hat was sodden and the rain was steadily licking down his collar.

"You write shit about Wales. This wonderful country..." he said, blinking in the rain and tailing off on a hoarse, emotional note.

Falstone frowned.

"For fuck's sake. You're going to hurt yourself. What the hell are you doing down there, anyway?"

"It's polluted."

"That's even more of a reason to stay away from it. Come on, you bloody idiot."

Falstone made his way towards him, steadying himself with tree limbs as Harry had done. When he was halfway down the bank, he stretched out his hand.

"Come on," Falstone said.

Harry clutched hold of his hand, squeezed it hard and pulled himself up. Falstone was doing a good job of assisting Harry when he slipped, taking Harry with him. They both spun, milling their arms wildly. Harry seemed to right himself in mid-air for a second before vanishing into the water. Falstone, without thinking, jumped in after him.

Chapter 26

Falstone, swirling and panting behind Harry, was getting closer. If it weren't for the weeks of torrential rain, the two of them might have been able to stand up. As it was, they were both sucked along, experiencing the same choking panic. Although Harry had never been great at swimming, his technique of attacking the water was instinctive. He grabbed for whatever he could and looked towards the banks. The stories he had written loomed larger. He was going to get out of this story. No journalist was going to sit before their Remington or Olivetti. No hardened hack was going to visit Bridget and request a photograph. He grabbed for a branch in the water and although it dislodged and came with him, it stabilised and calmed him. Falstone caught up with Harry, who had never been so happy to see someone else in his life. Together, the pair were able to paddle and wriggle, using the current to reach a natural low bank.

Falstone clawed his way out of the water with surprising power. The Fleet Street journalist held onto Harry's wrist for a second while he caught his breath. He seemed to know that the old man wouldn't have it in him to pull himself up. The water swirled around Harry's shoulders and he felt his clothes pulling him down. He thought about trying to get his shoes off, but he was worried Falstone might lose his grip. The Fleet Street journalist gave himself a couple of minutes to recover and then pulled from a squatting position until Harry's shoulders were clear of the river; he pulled and levered and dragged him until he was out of the water.

Harry lay on the bank as Falstone collapsed down next to him with an exhausted sigh and punched his shoulder in a comradely fashion. He had ceased to think and he hardly heard anything above his chattering teeth. He would talk to Falstone later. And he would thank him properly.

On the opposite bank, someone appeared. A policeman joined them and shouted across to find out how they were doing. Did they need an ambulance? Falstone replied that they needed dry clothes and to get warm.

"Thanks," Harry said after a time.

"Don't worry about it. You'd have done the same for me."

Harry looked at Falstone to see whether he was being ironic. He was.

"Quite a story," Falstone said.

"No. God no."

Harry was too exhausted to say anything more.

"'Fleet Street Journalist Comes to the Rescue of Local Reporter'?"

Harry thought about it. He didn't really care, but there was something funny about him covering the Taff as if it were improving and then falling into the filth. Perhaps he'd been too quick to judge the man who had come to his rescue. Perhaps Falstone's authoritative manner that had riled him at the disaster was experience rather than arrogance. That's what people put down to karma, thought Harry. It all came back to the village and the day of the disaster.

He realised he hadn't really moved on from that story. He remembered Evan's warnings about getting stuck in the past and wondered whether it was something to do with his age. So many old-timers at the Canton Male Voice Choir were nostalgic. Perhaps it was time for him to retire, although the thought of it scared him. A lump formed in his throat and he fought back tears as he lay in the mud. Everything felt like it was either spiralling out of control or already over. Pulling himself together lest Falstone see, Harry told himself that perhaps he could write a column, develop a space to publish whatever he wanted. He struggled to a sitting position and hugged himself. He would think about it all later.

At that moment, two policemen arrived holding grey blankets.

"We absolutely stink. I don't want to think of what," Falstone said.

"I could tell you, but I think you'd prefer not to know," Harry whispered through chattering teeth. It came back to him then, everything he had heard from the Glamorgan River Authority. He shivered to think of it: the ammonia, the tar, the acids and the faecal organisms. "I'm not even sure which would kill us quicker: drowning in it or drinking it."

Chapter 27

A few days after the river incident, Harry paced up and down in his living room, just having banished the large brass mantel clock to the cupboard under the stairs and slammed the door. It might have been saying 'tut, tut, tut' rather than 'tick, tick, tick', and the hollow, rhythmic sound had been driving him mad. He paced for a further five minutes before deciding that it was stupid to allow himself to be tormented. He retrieved the ornament and returned it to the mantel, grimacing as he did so.

Harry had lost more than his job. Something within himself was different and had been for some time, but he couldn't articulate anything specific. He held a vague feeling of simultaneous loss and repair, as if he had just realised his appendix was missing after suddenly noticing a fully healed scar. When had his appendix, so to speak, been taken? When had the recovery taken place? These tricky insubstantial non-questions were precisely why he didn't want to sit around at home. He was interrogating himself on matters he knew nothing about and yet he was the only one who had any hope of forming answers. He was trying to have a conversation with a side of him that was quite shut up. Perhaps he had finally let go of imagining himself as the father of a family. That seemed like the logical answer, but he still wasn't sure whether it was the right one, and it didn't explain why he felt a healing had taken place when he was, in fact, more isolated than ever.

The light streaming in the windows had an empty, depressing and eerie quality. Harry's current state was a forerunner of what retirement would feel like: ghostly, divorced and lonely. Everything was unbearably depressing. On the rare occasions he left the house, his gaze was downcast. He wanted to avoid the outside and any associates he might bump into, but he knew that remaining indoors was a trap. He shut the curtains; the light did nothing for his mood.

The mornings were the worst. Time seemed to stretch and stretch ahead. He would sit and read or stare out the window for hours, his teeth clamped together, his brows knitted. He began to fret about small things in his home which had never bothered him before. He wondered about work. What was Julian up to? What was the latest scoop? He missed the thrill of knowing and discussing the news hours before anyone else.

In the days after the memorial service, confining himself to his home, Harry had scanned the national papers looking for the rescue article written by Falstone, but it never appeared. Combing through had made him feel sicker than when he had ingested the Taff, but Falstone, for his own reasons, hadn't published. Not only did Harry have an overwhelming sense of gratitude growing towards the man he had hated, but the fact that he'd decided not to publish brought on a new level of respect. Harry wondered at first and then became wholly convinced that Falstone shared with him many similarities; this was owed to the Fleet Street journalist's presumed sensitivity in not running the story. Harry felt a brotherly solidarity towards him, even conceding that Paul Falstone might actually applaud his exposé once it was published. There was a loud rapping at his front door. He wasn't sure whether to answer it. It was an unfriendly knock. Hard and brisk.

It was Julian. There was no smile or greeting. He refused tea and sat in the chair opposite Harry's on the other side of the fire. It wasn't that cold outside and Julian tugged at his coat in the heat of the room.

"Bloody hell, it's hot!"

"I think I've got a bit of a chill. Have you been in work?"

"Yes."

"What are they saying?"

Julian gave no answer but simply stared into the fire. Harry was longing to know everything that was going on. When Julian finally spoke, it was in a different direction.

"What the hell did you think you were doing?"

Julian fumbled in his coat pocket for his cigarette carton. He held the end of a cigarette on the red, glowing bars of the fire and Harry noticed Julian's hands shaking slightly as the tip slowly toasted. Julian had to take a few deep drags to get it going, tense and impatient, sucking his cheeks in. Unsatisfied, he put the tip back on the fire, generating a few small sparks. Only when it was well lit, did he then repeat his question. The boy seemed even angrier now than he had been after Harry's accident. Something else, Harry assumed, must be bothering the lad.

"I don't know," Harry said, watching Julian closely. "If you'd been there when it first happened, you'd understand. I wanted to keep the village out of the press or the press out of the village."

"We're supposed to be objective."

Harry laughed cynically.

"There is no such thing as objectivity, Julian. You'll learn, especially if you end up in Fleet Street. We pick what goes in and what doesn't. The things that drive us, timing of editions and the amount of space in the paper, these things get in the way of the facts. All the time we're making choices: this headline or that introduction. I went too far. Of course I did..."

"Yes—"

"Think about it. The London press are manipulating the stories about Aberfan. They write about bitterness and suspicion and then people in the village start to wonder. They read the paper and see it not for the muckraking sensationalism that it is, but as a mirror. They think these journalists in Fleet Street are objective. I don't want to hold that funhouse mirror up to a village which has been through enough."

"You should have talked to me."

"Julian, we're talking now. Who is the real villain of Aberfan?"

"The NCB."

"Exactly. But that's not the narrative any longer. The fairy tale of Fleet Street is that if your child survived, you can't trust the bereaved. If your child died, you can't trust the parents of survivors. Everyone covets either your money or your child. Once suspicion and mistrust grew, the Aberfan villagers started to be demonised in the press as unhinged with greed and jealousy. People who had generously donated to the Disaster Fund are reading these stories and wishing they hadn't. Where is the NCB in all this?"

"Forgotten," Julian agreed.

"It's textbook divide and conquer."

"But you behaved no better than Doxsey with *Ulysses*. He didn't want people to see the film and you didn't want them reading about Aberfan."

"It's completely different."

"No, it's not. The tragedy is, once upon a time, you would have rejoiced about Doxsey. When you finally get the chance to pin something on a corrupt councillor... I'm not even sure what you achieved."

"Maybe that's because it hasn't all played out yet."

"Are you still planning a piece about Fleet Street? Evan told me he won't go for it."

"Wait until he's read it. Once he has, things will get back to normal."

"You mean he'll have you back?"

"That's the plan. What have they said in work?"

"Nothing. Nobody's mentioning it."

"Who are you working with?"

"Christ, Harry, do you have to keep it so hot in here?"

Harry raised his eyebrows and waited.

"I've got to work with George."

"Is he giving you a hard time?"

"She looks happy," Julian said, and he picked up a black and white picture of Bridget, aged about forty, from the tiled mantelpiece.

It had been taken on a beachfront, but it couldn't have been warm because she was wearing a check winter coat. She was beaming at someone out of shot and leaning forwards from the waist, feet together. Julian sensed from her expression and the lean that she may have been calling to a dog or child near the photographer.

"Look, I'm sorry if I caused you worry. I really am," Harry said, taking the picture from Julian and putting it back. "She was furious with me – about the accident at the river."

"What did she say?"

"There wasn't much she didn't. Called me an old fool. Said I could have been killed. I thought she was going to throw something. She was very upset."

"She cares about you."

Harry looked at the picture. Julian was right – her face was beaming.

"I didn't realise," he said. "Maybe that's my fault. I never asked."

"What are you going to do?"

"Salvage something, if she wants me to. That's what I'm trying to do with everything else; I need to salvage something."

Harry turned up for choir in no mood for singing, but neither was he in the mood for sitting at home reflecting. He was surprised to find Idris there early, with the other Welsh Office workers. They all waved a cordial hello to Harry. He gave a clipped smile and talked to some of the retired old-timers. Harry found the first half dragged, resolved as he was to speak to Idris during the break, but as he watched the grey and white heads following the conductor, he wondered why he should bother. They weren't the only choir in the world; leaving was an option. The hands of the clock seemed to twitch endlessly in the same position. Harry wondered why he had felt such a tie to them and why it had blinded him to the bigger picture. Finally, he saw one of the tenors slide from the group and put the kettle on.

"Idris, I need to speak to you," he said, grabbing the civil servant as the collective broke up.

"It's just politics, Harry. It's nothing personal. Don't worry about it."

Idris waved a hand, brushing away the past.

"It was your own fault," Harry retorted.

"You're still going on about that? The memorial service is over. We needed to make Wales sound a bit nicer. They were destroying us. Did you see the article the *Sunday Express* wrote about us? Selwyn wrote a letter of complaint, but they wouldn't even publish it. Wouldn't even publish the damn thing. If we learned anything from Wilson, it's that you can't bloody ask the press directly for their cooperation. God, no. That's asking too much. We had to be a bit more subtle. I'm sorry you lost your job, old chap. You were in agreement with us, weren't you? We didn't ask you to do anything that you didn't want to. Fleet Street was your idea. The Lay Off Aberfan campaign was your idea. And both turned out to be great disappointments."

"What was the truth about Paul Falstone?"

"I guess you've heard, then."

"That he wasn't even in Wales until the memorial service?"

"But that's not to say that there weren't unscrupulous Fleet Street journalists stirring up those two fathers."

"I don't need to be spoon-fed. It was a distraction in the end. One I could have done without."

"Harry, we've thought about it and we're extending an invitation for you to join us at the Welsh Office. We can't be more welcoming than that. What's the alternative? You'll go back to writing those awfully depressing pieces about the Taff, the lack of employment and the fact that they're shutting the mines. You were making Wales look simply terrible."

"I was making Wales look terrible? Those letters you wrote to Downing Street, the BBC and *The Telegraph* make you look bloody provincial."

"Wilson can't talk."

Harry shrugged and pondered on the wider significance of their response to the disaster. Since television came onto the scene, image was everything in political life. Wasn't it that which had brought Wilson victory in the first place? The Prime Minister had been every bit at home in the TV studio as he was with Parliament.

Break over, they sang again as one, but it would be for the last time. Harry felt he had bigger things to take care of. He understood that the Welsh Office did their best in all ways to project a picture-perfect image of Wales. He came to think that the Welsh hymns weren't hymns of the past so much as prayers for the future. Weeks later, Harry tried out at a new group: Cardiff Athletic Male Choir. If Harry had sought to cut all ties with the Welsh Office, he couldn't have found a more apt way to demonstrate the new direction. Thereafter, the old boys of the Welsh Office wouldn't have given him a story even if he begged.

Chapter 28

This is going to go off like a grenade tossed down Fleet Street, Harry thought.

Sitting at his kitchen table, the blue Underwood again in front of him, Harry applied himself to writing the best article he could on the Aberfan memorial service and how the London press had done their best to distort and falsify the truth. His focus was on the *Daily Express* and *The Daily Telegraph*, but they were by no means exclusively accountable. Harry had fact-checked with the Press Association. He had telephoned the journalists involved in a number of the stories. Harry felt a great sense of something larger than himself at work. He was being pushed towards something significant, though unable to guess at the specifics or the outcome.

He told himself he was going to get his job back. The way Fleet Street reported news would be changed forever. The room vanished and his thoughts rattled along with the speed of his typing. His spirits were lifting the more he typed. He could write his way back in. His exile was almost over and he appreciated his job more than ever before. When he finished the article, he read it through, delighting that it was far more hard-hitting than he had anticipated. Written down, the story was absolutely scandalous. It would be the talk of London's media.

Delivering his work to Thomson House turned out to be far easier than he had thought. For a start, he had imagined rather melodramatic ideas about being stopped in reception, and he had worried that his colleagues might give him a hard time, or that he might have to endure the snide comments of the *Western Mail* staff. However, the receptionist greeted him like an old friend. Harry wasn't sure whether he was imagining it or not, but she seemed to welcome him with a touch of sympathy. There was no one around on the first floor. He simply walked into Evan's empty office and left the story on his desk. He glanced back at it and took a deep breath before resolutely nodding to himself and leaving. Achieving a safe exit proved to be trickier. Huw met Harry as he was passing through the newsroom. Immediately, Huw launched into telling Harry that he was missed, but Harry raised his hand to signal him to stop talking and stared into the middle distance as if lost in thought.

"Did you hear that?" Harry asked.

"What?"

"Wait. Where's Julian?"

"I'm not sure." Huw scanned the newsroom. "He was with George a minute ago."

Harry kept quiet and listened. A phone began to ring, but there had definitely been the sound of a raised voice in the corridor.

"Harry," Huw said. "I think—"

"I'll be back now."

"You don't work here any more," Huw said, more to himself than Harry.

Already making his way towards the shouting, Harry was out of earshot as Huw cursed George and his temper. Harry burst through the door into the corridor and turned some corners before confronting exactly the scene he had imagined. George was nose to nose with Julian, who was pressed against the wall. Clutched in George's hand was a sheaf of crumpled newspaper.

"Just the fucking man," George said to Harry. "Ask your fucking protégé what he's done today."

"What's going on here?"

"Do you realise what was on that page?" George said with his teeth gritted, but at least he was moving away from Julian.

"I do now," Julian said, sliding further away from George.

"Woe betide you if it happens again. The same column repeated twice on the same page? Unforgivable. Once is enough for anyone to be in the paper for a crime. Watch your back, my boy."

"You watch yours!" Harry said.

"Weren't you fucking fired? Haven't you got another conspiracy theory to write up? What's it this time? Fleet Street killed Kennedy?"

"Don't start that collection just yet."

George, confused, returned to the newsroom. Julian sank back against the wall with a sigh.

"What the hell was that all about?" Harry asked him.

Julian shrugged.

"Don't give it another thought," Harry assured him. "You'll be working with me again soon enough. I've written something quite brilliant. There isn't a doubt in my mind that Evan will have me back when he's read it."

The depth of Harry's feelings when he realised the boy was in trouble had surprised him.

"You missed the outcome of the Doxsey case," Julian said, unsure about how to respond to Harry's hint that they would be colleagues again.

Harry wondered why the young man looked so grim.

"How long did he get?"

"They were all acquitted, Harry."

"They were all what?"

"The judge hinted to the jury that they should let him off."

"They ignored Mary Hallinan?"

"Completely."

Harry couldn't believe how big this was. He asked Julian for the name of the judge. The corruption spread all the way to the top. The city was contaminated with it. These people had networks which made them untouchable. Harry assured Julian that he would turn over the Conservative Mr Justice Paull when he was back in his job, but Julian hadn't finished.

"And now fifteen similar trials have collapsed. The Cardiff trial was set up to be legal precedence, but now it's a cautionary tale. They're all scared to have anything to do with councillors."

"Unbelievable! It's impossible."

Julian frowned and Harry grabbed him by the shoulders and looked him in the eyes.

"You see what I mean? Do you understand what we do now – as journalists? What we try to do? At least you've seen it for yourself now. We have an important role and sometimes we succeed and sometimes we fail, but we keep trying. We fight for social justice where sometimes legal justice fails us entirely."

"Of course," he said.

Another very small consolation to Harry was that the *Ulysses* debate was rumbling on. Julian had gone to Caerphilly the previous day to interview councillors who had allowed, by a vote of eleven to nine, that *Ulysses* play in their cinemas. Harry could not wait for the reinstatement he believed was coming. Just hearing about what he'd missed filled him with longing. Julian hesitatingly confessed that he might have helped Doxsey's secretary, Annie, land a job in the tele-ads department and asked Harry not to get wound up about it. They were dating, but it was all above board, he assured his old mentor. Harry didn't care. He was almost at the point of not caring if Doxsey himself landed a job in the canteen; he just wanted to return himself. As Harry and Julian continued to talk, Evan came around the corner and stopped short. Harry's exposé was in his hands.

"Harry, you don't work here. I need you to leave."

"But have you read it?"

"Yes, I've read it. You're out of your fucking mind. I need you to leave or I'll have to have you seen out."

Evan thrust the papers at Harry's chest, forcing him to take them back. Harry knew not to go any further because Evan looked positively furious. He wanted to ask why he was so angry or at least discuss it with him, but the tone with which the words had been delivered told him it was futile. Harry, confused, left the building rubbing his chin as though Evan had actually punched him. Julian followed Harry to the top of the stairs and watched him go, unable to think of a single thing to say and unsure as to what had just happened. Harry wouldn't have heard, anyway. He was far too deeply shocked. It didn't make any sense to him. His story was ground-breaking. It was in the public interest. All that he could think of was that he had been wrong. The scale of how badly things had gone wrong was incalculable, at least for the moment. His whole plan seemed as though it had always been doomed to failure, but he had been so certain of success. The exposé was the finest, most honest and true thing he'd ever written.

Feeling lightheaded and dry in the mouth, he walked along Wood Street in the direction of Tudor Street. With sudden clarity, he doubted his Fleet Street exposé would have caused the change he'd desired. Harry didn't berate himself for trying but instead wondered what direction he would have been more successful in. He regretted not having passed more on to Julian. At least he could have affected one person for the better.

He stopped on the bridge overlooking the Taff, attracting a few stares. Harry was quite unaware of himself. He was drained of colour and his gaze appeared to be inward, searching for something. Finally, with a little shake of his head, he abandoned his reflections and leaned over the rail. Looking at the water far below, he unclasped his fingers and let the pages he'd been holding flutter and twist down to the surface. Harry crossed the road and looked up towards Taffs Mead Embankment as the pages floated underneath the bridge. He wished the river would hurry and speed his story to oblivion, but it flowed languid and unrushed. The paper undulated with the water. His thoughts traced the course that the polluted river had taken through Bute Park and Pontcanna Fields; the Long Wood and Morganstown, overlooked by Castell Coch; Gwaelod-y-Garth,

Treforest and the edge of St Gwynno Forest; Abercynon, before which the river had looped Quakers Yard and Aberfan.

He thought of the power in that small mountain spring. The NCB had even known of its presence but considered it to be an insignificant risk. The black teardrop, saturated over a long period of years, had existed in a fragile and tremulous state as though it were a real tear poised on the edge of an eyelid. Then came the endless rain.

The key factor had been time.

For small things to make a big difference, you need time. Harry considered that he hadn't been given enough. He recalled Tom's words of advice. Persuading one editor or journalist to lay off would have made no difference. The thoughts of Tom brought him back to Fleet Street. He'd wanted to teach them a lesson. Not just for Aberfan – unforgivable journalistic behaviour and reporting in itself – but for the way he'd been sacked because of his loyalty, for trying to help a colleague. But he'd missed a step in his efforts. He hadn't succeeded in anything other than writing a few less stories. Had his embarrassment on the day of the Aberfan disaster given him a phantom audience to win over? The only people who'd noticed at all were the Welsh Office and, at the cost of Harry's career, his editor. If he had wanted to change things, he couldn't have done worse than water down his true feelings or try to make them invisible.

As he started trudging slowly towards home, the tearstained face of the young mother in the cinema, caught in the photographer's Fleet Street flash, came to mind again. What was more truthful? And what, for that matter, was the alternative? A photograph of a bereaved mother stoically buttering bread with the Civil Defence ladies? A village getting over their terrible loss with profound dignity? A clean river and cleaner politics in the picture-postcard land of song?

Later, sat in his armchair and still reflecting on the events of the day, he was aware of a car in the street pulling up followed by the slam of its door. When he heard his letterbox lift and something weighty land on the mat, he got up. He'd been about to check what had arrived, tense with the thought of more bad news, when the sound of the car starting up again made him run back to the front window. He tore back the nets with deliberate aggression in the hope that whoever it was would know they'd been spotted. He saw Evan raise a hand in acknowledgement before driving off. Perhaps, thought Harry, he's reconsidered and wants me back.

After rushing to the front door, Harry found a folded copy of the Echo with an envelope containing two references, one from Evan and one from Mr Taylor. Mr Taylor's reference focused on his length of service at the Echo, while Evan's reference described him as one of the best journalists he'd worked with.

Harry turned his attention to the newspaper, in which he spotted a small advert circled in red. It was almost too small to be legible. He took the paper back into the living room, stood by the window and lifted the nets to allow him as much light to read in as possible.

CARDIFF JOURNALISM SCHOOL. Applications are welcome from suitably qualified people for the post of LECTURER IN JOURNALISM. Role to teach the subjects of newspaper practice and ethics to professional level and also to develop short courses on suitable topics related to Journalism. Duties to commence on 1st January 1968, or as soon as possible thereafter. Salary (under review) starting at £1,875, depending on age and experience. Applications, together with the names and addresses of two referees, should be sent to Mr Cowie, Cardiff Journalism School, Colchester Avenue, Cardiff.

Harry looked in the direction of Evan's car and smiled. 'When you pass through the waters I will be with you; and through the rivers, they shall not overwhelm you', he recalled.

Author's Note

In the months after the Aberfan disaster, the Welsh Office became deeply concerned about press intrusion. The Welsh Office sent a letter to Downing Street dated 22 September 1967. Hoping that Downing Street would exercise control over the London press, it contained a number of suggestions for the Government, of which the following is one example:

"Newspapers, generally, increased their sales at the time of the disaster at Aberfan. A single newspaper (e.g. the *Mirror*) might well increase its sales on a more lasting basis by starting a 'Lay Off Aberfan' campaign. We are confident that such a campaign would ultimately receive the support of newspapers and broadcasting organisations throughout the land."

Acknowledgements

I would like to thank the following people and organisations for their assistance and support:

Present and former *Echo/Western Mail/Merthyr Express* editors, reporters and subs who gave up their valuable time for interviews: Martin Shipton, Mike Thomas, Roger Morrissey, John Cosslett, Tony Sicluna, John Humphries, Phillip Nifield, Bram Humphries (and the Wednesday Clubbers), Rowland Davies (whose mother's basement is filled with enough literary resources to rival the National Library of Wales) and Brian Lee (who was particularly generous regarding information on 1960s Cardiff).

Myrddin ap Dafydd of Gwasg Carreg Gwalch, Petra Bennett of Literature Wales, Lucy Thomas of the Welsh Books Council and Phil Carradice.

Gwen Davies and Daniel Leeman for their speedy and meticulous editing.

Enormous thanks to the truly talented South Wales artist Sarah Richards for creating the beautiful, moving and yet dignified cover image.

Dr Richard Lewis and Mr John Jenkins of the BMA, Professor Bob Franklin, I C Rapoport, Rachel Davies of Martyn Prowel Solicitors, David John Evans, Alexander Cooper, Merthyr Library, Cardiff Central Library, the National Library of Wales, Swansea Miners' Library, the Richard Burton Archives at Swansea University and the National Archives.

The story was inspired by Welsh Office correspondence I found at the National Archives and Idris Evans of the Information Division has occasionally been quoted directly in speech. I have also drawn from articles published in the *South Wales Echo* in the aftermath of the Aberfan disaster and articles focussing on the activities of Sidney Doxsey, a Cardiff Tory councillor. For further information on this novel and the research that informed it, please visit its website (www.blackriver.cymru).